BORN
Lucky

—H. L. Seibel—

A Bowstring Production
—Independence, Missouri—

WITH APPRECIATION TO
JOHN LARSON & ISAIAH JOHNSON
FOR READING THIS MORE THAN ONCE.

PUBLISHED BY

BOWSTRING PRODUCTIONS
—INDEPENDENCE, MISSOURI—

COVER DESIGN COURTESY OF RENAN SCHEFFER

3RD PRINTING: 2026
ISBN: 978-0-9905325-0-7

♦

Here it is, Melissa—
the story I was
telling you about…
I tell myself you would
have liked it…

♥

BORN
Lucky

ENTER THE JOKER

Some people are born lucky.

"Excuse me—miss? I'd like a refill on my—miss? Excuse me?"

I am not one of them. I mean to say—I couldn't even snag the attention of my waitress.

And yet, there was a time when I thought that I could, by sheer effort of will, thwart the fates.

The hollow laugh.

The rueful snort.

I couldn't thwart the lid off a paper bag. If paper bags had lids. Which they don't.

What I mean to say is that one cannot, one eventually discovers, escape one's destiny.

The colorless sigh.

My attention strayed to the young couple at a nearby table. Hers was an oval face, framed in dark curls; his was the collegiate look that girls find so irresistible.

No wonder her every glance was a caress, her every word a sonnet, her touch heaven.

I rose abruptly, dumped some coins on the table and headed for the door—

At the door a clumsy bloke with red hair and a great-coat failed to see me. I was knocked to the floor.

Seriously!

I lay there.

Winded.

Stunned.

But it was more than that. After all, what was the point? If every journey was doomed, if every opportunity was a guaranteed loss, if every deck was stacked—well, just what exactly was the bloody point?

Beefy hands reached down. "Sorry about that, bud."

I stared.

The words were addressed to me.

No one ever addressed words to me.

I was helped to my feet. My jacket was swiped at with great, broad strokes.

Unprecedented.

"Sebastian!" cried the boyish grin, thrusting out the meaty paw and introducing himself. "Sebastian, uh, Smith!"

Bluff.

Hearty.

Infernally jovial.

I imagined people flocked to him like bees to honey.

"I'm Phil." I was still reeling. My cloak of invisibility had, inexplicably, been rent. "I mean Philadelphia. My name is Philadelphia Potts."

"Let me buy you a drink, Philadelphia Potts!"

I nearly fell down again.

"Me?" I croaked.

He propelled me to a table.

Waitresses appeared.

Smiling.

Eager.

Helpful.

Another world entirely.

I batted away the self-pitying tear.

And gave myself over to basking in the presence of one of the lucky ones.

1

It wasn't until the poker game that I found out just how blamed lucky Sebastian was.

I tried, of course, to avoid the game. I wanted no part in an endeavor in which luck played even the tiniest part.

"No, no," I protested. "Really. No. Thanks, but no. No."

"Nonsense!"

Cards were dealt. Waitresse s who had, moments before, been eagerly attentive, now feigned ignorance admirably—private games were frowned upon.

I played.

I lost.

Nickels and dimes I really couldn't spare exchanged hands.

"Really," I protested weakly. "No more."

Sebastian chuckled and dealt the cards.

Like trying to say no to a tsunami.

"Don't feel bad." His grin was contagious. "I guess you might say I was born lucky."

The inner laugh.

Bitter and biting.

I could tell him a thing or two about luck—none of it good.

I sighed and listlessly thumbed through my cards.

I stopped breathing.

Emptied my pockets onto the table.

Sebastian lifted the inquiring eyebrow.

"Something—call it a premonition, a hunch—something tells me you think quite a lot of your hand." The tone was playful, engaging.

I swallowed hard and nodded vigorously.

His grin belied the rueful shaking of his head. "The thing is—the thing you should know—is this: I cannot lose."

"If I had more—I'd bet it!" I cried impulsively.

My days of playing poker had been relatively few—I had not yet perfected the art of the disingenuous approach.

He gave me the contemplative look.

"You don't believe me, do you?"

I shook my head.

He shoved a piece of paper my way. "I'll take an I.O.U."

Wild hope yanked away my breath. "Any amount?"

He gave a careless shrug.

With a hand that shook like a man palsied, I scrawled a figure on the piece of paper.

His eyebrows went up.

"Perhaps," he appeared to be giving the matter some consideration, "I should fold."

"No!" I yelped.

He chuckled good-naturedly. "The thing is," he felt it necessary to remind me, "I can't be beaten."

"Chicken?" I pushed the word out, rusty from disuse.

"Not at all," he said generously. The disarming grin was back. "Besides, it's your funeral." He initialed the paper.

With something of a flourish, I displayed my cards.

"A royal flush," he murmured. "Now there's something you don't see every day." He laid down a sea of nines, added a joker. "Pity five of a kind trumps a royal flush."

I went hot and cold by turns.

He collected and rifled the cards. "You must be extraordinarily unlucky, losing with a hand like that. Again?"

I wondered how deep the river was.

He fingered his chin. "The river," he said, suggesting that on top of everything else he possessed mind-reading capabilities, "isn't your best bet. With your luck you'd either be rescued, or you'd find it wasn't as deep as you expected. Either way, deuced uncomfortable." He drummed his fingers on the table. "Perhaps you'd care to do me a favor instead?"

I raised my eyes to his, tried to focus.

He pushed a black medical bag across the table at me. His manner became businesslike. "There's a girl I'd like you to—" He drew a finger across his throat. "I don't care how. Don't want to know, really. But if you find yourself running short on ideas, as I suspect you will, you'll find a revolver in here. Loaded.

"She will think you're just another doctor," he continued, oblivious to the consternation running rampant across my face, "to care for her dying grandfather."

I worked the jaws. "I can't—" I protested hoarsely. "I mean, really—I can't! See, I—I—I—I can't. I just can't," I finished lamely.

The smile did not quite reach his eyes. "No, I am sure you cannot," he mused. He seemed to have drifted off, and for a moment I wasn't sure if he was still talking to me or if he had entered a realm beyond my vision. "No one can. But you'll make the attempt. And should you succeed," he concluded briskly, flattening his hands, "no more I.O.U."

Confusion clouded my eyes.

"Never mind," he said, his good humor restored.

"Your train leaves in forty minutes. Ticket's in the bag. So are your directions. Grandfather's medications are clearly labeled. Make no mistake—it is imperative that you administer them accordingly! Lucky for me I ran into you."

"But—! But I—! I—!" I protested, sensing I was floundering in waters deeper than the river could possibly have afforded.

"The river," he said pointedly, "will be here when you return."

A force far superior to mine propelled me out the door.

2

The world rushed past. I was being swept along by an evil and unforgiving tide, the black bag on my knees my unlikely anchor. My hands gripped the handle, white-knuckled. My thoughts were jumbled and incoherent.

Meaningless.

Luck, always my nemesis, had shown her true colors at last. The perplexities and annoyances of life had simply been Luck's way of toying with her prey. This was Luck with her claws unsheathed and her fangs bared.

A woman with three chins and a monstrous hat entered the compartment. She groaned onto the seat next to me.

"I see you're a doctor!" she wheezed.

I looked at her, vaguely troubled.

She shifted. "Lumbago," she explained. Or maybe she said "gout." Not that it mattered. She wasn't talking to me—she was talking to my black bag.

The inevitable sigh and a slumping of the shoulders as she launched into a detailed catalogue of her ailments.

There's no fighting Luck.

The compartment door banged open. "Is there a—you! Doctor! Come quick!"

"Me?" I said, confused.

"You!"

"I'm not a doctor."

"Off you go, young man," said Three Chins, prodding me with a slab of meat that was her elbow.

"I'm not a doctor."

Ignored.

I stumbled along.

3

The girl was in the dining car, standing in the aisle, one hand at her throat, the other stretched upwards, as though to grasp something only she could perceive. Her face was mottled, and her eyes looked like they were trying to roll back in her head. She was trying, with absolutely no success whatsoever, to breathe. Drool spilled out of her mouth. Unfortunate noises issued from her. She swayed.

Men and women clustered round watching, spellbound, the insidious approach of certain death.

"Make way for the doctor!"

People reluctantly parted.

For me.

Rather, for the black bag.

It was unnerving.

I looked at the girl. Me, I'm not good with girls. They scare me. Intimidate me. Gasping, choking, dying girls, I quickly discovered, are a thousand times worse.

"Uh," I said.

"Save her!" commanded Three Chins, who had followed.

I set the black bag down to wipe my brow. I raised my hand to steady myself on the curtain rod.

It wasn't a curtain rod.

It was a cord.

I accidentally pulled it.

Brakes squealed. The train lurched. The girl was thrown against me. She knocked me down.

Landed on top of me.

Something shot out of her mouth and got all over my shirt.

A girl.

On top of me.

She was breathing.

Ragged and labored—

But breathing.

A girl.

I was conscious of a great peace. The peace deepened as her coloring returned to normal.

Her eyes focused.

They were hazel.

She smiled.

I stopped breathing.

"Sorry," she said.

There was a musical quality about her voice that made my insides lurch.

She rose, removing her delicious weight, her warmth, her nearness.

She extended her hand and I wondered at it. Fumbled my hand into it. Her skin was smooth and soft.

She helped me to my feet, gently wiped at my shirt, straightened my collar. The crowd lost interest and melted away. "I guess I owe you my life," she murmured.

I wobbled my lips, but nothing came out.

She granted me another smile.

It brought the blood thundering to my head.

"By the way, I'm Andelucia," she said. "Pleased to meet you."

The world shuddered in its course.

Luck had once again played me for the fool.

I had, inadvertently and incomprehensibly, saved the very girl I had been sent to—

I couldn't finish the thought.

4

"Do you believe in coincidence?"

I found the question vaguely disturbing. Luck I believed in. Luck I understood to the uttermost.

I wasn't so sure about coincidence.

I considered again the thing which I had been commissioned to do. It was madness, of course.

Unthinkable.

I couldn't do it.

But then a vision appeared before my eyes, an unbidden glimpse of my I.O.U.

A wall of numbness enclosed my mind.

I reached into the bag.

Andelucia dropped the vehicle into a lower gear, pointed us towards the sky, and trod heavily upon the accelerator. We had, since our unconventional introduction—and the slight unpleasantness regarding the braking of the train—arrived at the station, disembarked, and continued our journey in her car. Now the last dregs of the setting sun turned her brown hair a rich gold, and the smile which seemed to hover perpetually on her lips illuminated her features.

The thing would have to be done quickly, if it were to be done at all.

"I don't," Andelucia continued breezily. "I don't think anything happens by coincidence. I think everything happens for a reason and there's a reason for everything that happens."

The wall became a fortress.

Impenetrable.

My hand found the weapon.

It was cold.

Heavy.

Repulsive.

I positioned it within the bag so that it was directed at the girl beside me.

Andelucia took her eyes off the road in order to flash me a quick smile. "Like you, snatching me from the arms of death. I don't think that was—are you okay?"

I had not meant to groan aloud.

"It's probably my driving," Andelucia was quick to apologize. "Sebastian says I'll be the death of someone yet. There! You see? I must have done it again! I'm so sorry!"

I gripped the gun a little tighter. "Sebastian," I said

tightly. "How well do you know this Sebastian?"

Andelucia gave me the enigmatic smile. "Pretty well, I'd say. Do you know what I think?" Her words were a pleasantly lilting melody that twisted the knife within my soul. "I think you're here for a reason! I—my, that was a rough patch of road, wasn't it? I think good things are going to start happening—and I'll tell you why: because you're here!"

She shot me a commiserating glance. "It's this bridge, isn't it? We've begged the county for years to repair it!"

It wasn't the bridge.

My hand trembled as my finger closed around the trigger.

Andelucia risked removing a hand from the wheel in order to impulsively touch my free arm. "We're awfully lucky to have you, you know," she said softly.

I stared at her.

That which I couldn't do was not an option.

5

"Actually," continued Andelucia conversationally, "it's lucky we met up at all. I only go into town once a month to do the shopping."

Lucky.

I closed my eyes.

As long as Andelucia lived, I couldn't go home. Going home would mean facing Sebastian, and that was something I could not do. So going home was not an option.

I opened my eyes.

Maybe I didn't need to go home. Not as long as Andelucia's grandfather needed a doctor.

"We've had a dozen doctors in the last six months." Andelucia gave me her slow, soft smile. "I guess that makes you doctor number thirteen. Lucky number thirteen."

I shuddered.

"I wouldn't be surprised if you had Grandfather up, hale and hearty, by the time Sebastian arrived."

I tightened my grip on the bag. "Sebastian? Here? Sebastian's coming here?"

"You'll be just fine," said Andelucia reassuringly. "My brother just likes to check in on us from time to time to see how the doctors he sends are doing. You'll be fine. Besides, you've already proved your mettle by saving my life."

I stared at her. "Sebastian's your brother? But he wants me to—he's your *brother?*"

Andelucia chuckled. "You'd be surprised at how often the doctors he sends react just like that. It's the color of our hair, isn't it? We don't look a thing alike. It's our parents' fault. Between the two of them they had about every bloodline you could imagine."

I closed my eyes.

Staying was not an option.

6

The house had probably been magnificent at one time. Gables and dormers and chimneys suggested a multitude of rooms; pillars and porches echoed the opulence of a bygone era. Ivy reaching to the third floor gave evidence of the passage of time.

In another place, in another time, such faded elegance would have given rest to my soul. Had I not been here under false pretenses the sight of such echoing magnificence would have thrilled me.

A girl of about seventeen spilled out of the house. The yellow sundress she wore was the color of her hair. Her smile was dimpled, her eyes blue.

"This is the new doctor, Daphne," said Andelucia.

Daphne was stunning.

My tongue failed to give utterance.

"Guess what, Andi! You'll never guess! Guess what!" cried Daphne.

She hadn't even noticed me.

Naturally.

Andelucia grabbed a couple bags of groceries. "Shouldn't you be watching Grandfather, Daphne?"

"Fishface called! He called, and guess what!"

I followed Andelucia into the house. We traversed a lengthy passage, past spacious rooms, sparsely furnished. Andelucia's frown deepened. "And why hasn't Clarissa set the table?"

"He said—!" cried Daphne portentously. "He said—and these are his exact words *exactly*—he said, 'Pray convey to Clarissa my earnest desire to speak with her on the morrow. I have something of particular importance to ask her.' That's exactly what he said, Andi!"

"Bianca!" demanded Andelucia abruptly. "Is Bianca in her room?"

"Do you know what I think?" Daphne pressed her hands to her chest and stopped dancing for two seconds in order to lend weight to her words. *"I think Fishface is going to propose!"*

The words were delivered in a breathless rush. Flashing eyes expressed excitement.

"And where's Evangeline?" Andelucia demanded.

"Andi!" wailed Daphne passionately. "Can't you listen to me for one minute? I'm trying to impress upon you something of vast importance and you're not even listening to me! I said—"

"Yes, Daphne," said Andelucia wearily. "I heard what you said. Besides, it's all over town that Frederick's had a run of bad luck, so a proposal was inevitable. Now go and bring in the rest of the groceries." She turned to me, and her slow, sweet smile blossomed. "It's just like I said, Doctor: I knew you'd bring us luck. Now, we'd better go see what mischief Evangeline is up to."

Daphne giggled. "I'd sure hate to be in Clarissa's shoes!"

7

It was at this juncture that the rather plain girl appeared. She was about fifteen, all sharp angles and flat planes, nearly as tall as Andelucia, with hair reddish in color, a nose generously spattered with freckles and a determined chin. There was a trowel in her hand and a smudge of dirt on her brow; she wore a pair of overalls, patched and soiled and in need of mending.

"There you are, Evangeline!" said Andelucia sharply. "Where's Bianca?"

Evangeline ignored the question. Gray eyes bored unexpectedly into me. "Is this the new doctor?"

I experienced a moment of dull surprise.

"I asked you a question, Evangeline!"

"Because he sure doesn't look like a doctor," said Evangeline, striking swiftly at the heart of the matter.

I shifted uneasily.

Andelucia snorted. "He saved my life, Evangeline."

"Did he?" The gray eyes were merciless. "What's in your bag, Doctor? What did you use to save her? Show us what you've got in there, Doctor!"

My grip on the black bag tightened.

"Evangeline!" said Andelucia sharply. "Leave the good doctor alone! Now where's Bianca?"

Evangeline reluctantly withdrew her disconcerting gaze from me. "In her room, Andi. Where did you think she was? Any mail for me?"

"Oh, dear," sighed Andelucia. "In the all the excitement I forgot to check."

"Andi!" wailed Evangeline.

"Go help your sister bring in the groceries," ordered Andelucia. She turned to me. "Come along, Doctor. We'd better go check on Grandfather."

I came along.

8

Grandfather didn't need a doctor. He needed a mortician. He was dead already, his face mottled and blotchy, a skin of rice paper stretched tightly over jagged bones.

"I'm home, Grandfather!" said Andelucia loudly, bending over the relic and giving him a quick peck on the cheek. "And I've brought the new doctor!"

Grandfather, defying the decree of an impartial Nature, drew a shallow, rattling breath.

"I think he's looking a little better," said Andelucia, straightening the covers and giving the withered head a pat. "The last doctor leached him before he—before he had to leave, and it's done him a world of good, don't you think?"

What I was thinking was that the tide was rising, and that the sooner I explained that I wasn't staying the better. My encounter with Evangeline had shaken me.

Besides, with Sebastian on his way it wasn't healthy for me to linger.

I cleared my throat.

"You'll sleep in here, so as to be close to Grandfather," said Andelucia.

The room she showed me was tucked in under the eaves. There was a bed, a chair, a small dresser, and another door opening onto the hall. On the dresser was a vase and in the vase were flowers, frail and delicate.

Andelucia smiled at me. "You can leave your bag here," she said.

I shook my head. My tongue felt thick and heavy. "I—I—"

Andelucia impulsively touched my arm. "Don't mind Daphne and Evangeline," she said. "They'll come around—just give them time."

Her ignorance was touching.

I found my voice. "I—I'm sorry you forgot to check for mail," I said.

It was not what I had intended to say. I had meant to tell her I was leaving. That I wouldn't be back. That I had a pressing appointment in town and that I was late already.

I think it was the flowers. It pleased me to think that Andelucia had put them there.

Andelucia's laughter was a brook in springtime. "Not to worry, Doctor. We never get anything of importance anyway. Let's eat!"

I deposited the black bag on the chair and dumbly followed.

9

It was difficult to eat.

Daphne's disturbing beauty.

Evangeline's brooding glances.

Andelucia's undeserved kindness.

And then, I nearly choked on my foul-tasting tea.

A girl a couple years older than Daphne swept into the room, the full train of a black-sequined evening dress rippling in her wake. Ropes of pearls drew attention to a plunging neckline and a diamond tiara sparkled atop her fine head. Ice-blonde hair fell down her back in glossy waves, emerald eyes gazed serenely at a point on the horizon, and a small, straight nose complemented an incorrigible mouth.

"Clarissa," said Andelucia, and a slight frown creased her brow, "this is the new doctor."

I lowered my spoon. Clearly and distinctly I spoke. "Meeting you is a hello."

Clarissa was profoundly attractive.

She failed entirely to acknowledge my existence.

Instead, she brought her attention down from its lofty estate and became intent upon a point somewhat past Andelucia's left ear. "Marry Frederick?" she said languidly, trailing her fingertips across the table. "I think not. I am going to marry a soldier boy, dashing and handsome in a new uniform." Her tone became dreamy. "He'll have been wounded, naturally, so I shall have to nurse him back to health. He will love me and I will love him."

Methought I heard the distant rumble of marching feet, as of young soldiers rushing off eagerly to get wounded.

Clarissa's manner became contemplative. "I do hope he doesn't have his legs blown off."

"Very well," returned Andelucia tartly. "Then I shall marry Frederick. You may have the responsibility of Grandfather and Bianca and Daphne and Evangeline, and I shall live a life of ease and luxury."

"No offense, Andi," Clarissa said, taking a seat next to Daphne with affected grace, "but next to me, Frederick wouldn't even look at you."

"Next to me either!" chimed in Daphne.

A dispassionate observer would have been forced to agree with these candid statements.

"None taken," said Andelucia dryly. "But let me

remind you that he'd even marry Evangeline in order to get his hands on his inheritance."

Evangeline stiffened.

"No offense, of course, Evangeline," murmured Andelucia.

Daphne hooted. "She's too young! He can't marry her!"

Clarissa fluttered a dismissive hand. "You have my blessing, Andi, dear."

Daphne clasped her hands. "We are going to be rich!" she gloated. "There will be butter at every meal and a new sash for my dress and more good things than you can count!"

Andelucia glanced at me apologetically. "Part of the arrangement is the settling of our debts," she explained. "Frederick's money is held in trust until he marries. We won't be rich, but we should have enough to enable us to—"

There came the sound of a footstep on the stair.

Conversation at the table ceased, and electricity seemed to surge through the room.

Clarissa raised a languid eyebrow. "I perceive someone has loosed Bianca." Her glance strayed to Evangeline. "Again."

Daphne giggled.

Evangeline's attention appeared to be wholly concerned with her tea. "Ick," she observed. "I think I put too much bitterroot in this batch."

"You do realize," Andelucia addressed Evangeline coolly, "that we're going to run out of doctors if you keep letting Bianca out. And when we run out of doctors, Grandfather will die. I will deal with you later, young lady."

Evangeline lifted reproachful eyes, and whether it was out of concern for her grandfather or for her impending punishment, it was impossible to tell.

Bianca came into view.

My soup spoon clattered to the table.

I wondered if my reason was toppling.

Because burned into my brain was an image of ivory, sculpted by a meticulous hand and molded with an eye toward unfathomable perfection.

Bianca was naked.

10

Once I had inadvertently glimpsed an expanse of a young woman's leg, owing to an unexpected gust of wind, and the delicacy of the shape had lived long in my memory, but this—

This was—

I stopped breathing and the room tilted dangerously.

"How droll," said Clarissa carelessly. "Here I've been laboring under the impression that we had confiscated all of Sebastian's guns."

There was a gun in Bianca's hand.

Funny I hadn't noticed it before. Funny, since it appeared to be pointed directly at me. Funny also since it appeared to be the one that Sebastian had put into the black bag.

"Can I call Sebastian and tell him we need a new doctor?" Daphne volunteered eagerly.

Evangeline snickered.

It was a perfectly reasonable question, since judging from Bianca's expression murder was next on the menu. She was looking straight at me, and if eyes are windows to the soul, then her soul was in the pit of hell. Never had I seen an expression so twisted with hatred, a visage so filled with malevolent fury. The apathy I had come to expect from the opposite sex was nothing compared to this new and raw emotion emanating from Bianca.

A besotted grin slid over my face and it became wonderfully apparent that my brain had severed all communication with me.

"I'll distract her, Doctor," hissed Andelucia. "I'll distract her while you take cover beneath the table."

It was amusing the way she thought I had control over my motor skills.

There came an imperceptible shift in Bianca's expression. Like ripples in a pond, perplexity and confusion moved across her face. She tilted her head, first this way, and then the other, and the way her blue-black hair brushed her shoulders was pure magic. She looked as though she was contemplating a hitherto unknown quantity. The world held its breath.

And then she lowered the gun. Almost absently, she laid it on the table.

Daphne's whisper was shrill and instant. "Did you see that? Did you see what Bianca just did? *She put the gun down!*"

"She didn't shoot him." Evangline sounded prodigiously disappointed.

"Curses," said Clarissa, and there was a peculiar note in her voice. "You know what this means, don't you?"

Daphne snorted. "It's not an omen, if that's what you're driving at!"

Clarissa's incorrigible mouth showed signs of petulance. "Has she ever *not* tried to kill a doctor?"

The words hardly registered; the narrowness of my escape was a matter of singular unimportance. I could not pull my eyes away from the vision standing at the end of the table.

"That doesn't mean it's an omen," said Daphne strongly. "I mean, if it *is* an omen, which it couldn't possibly be, well, I mean—really! What could it possibly portend?"

"It portends that I'm supposed to marry Frederick." Clarissa's voice was hollow. She sighed the martyr's sigh.

Daphne brightened. "We're going to be rich! Butter with every meal! Sashes! Good things all over the place!"

"What about your soldier boy?" Evangeline demanded. "Who's going to nurse your soldier boy back to health? Are you going to just sit back and watch him die?"

Clarissa pursed her lips. "Maybe Frederick will break his leg."

I stopped breathing. Bianca was moving towards me. She was moving towards me and it was like watching the breeze move through summer wheat.

Like sunlight dancing on water.

Like—

I wrenched my gaze from her.

Clarissa was staring at me. There was a thoughtful, contemplative look in her eye that I found singularly unnerving, so I shifted my gaze to Daphne, who was lost in a happy world in which butter and sashes were to be had in abundance.

And then the chair next to mine scraped the floor. There was a knife-hot awareness of Bianca seating herself next to me, and then further scraping as the distance between our chairs narrowed—I caught a glimpse of pearl-white thighs, their elegant contours altering as they came to rest on the chair.

"She's—she's sitting next to—to *him!*" Daphne's urgent whisper could be heard throughout the room.

"An omen," said Clarissa mournfully, and she glared at me as though to suggest that I was somehow to blame.

"Something's wrong with Bianca," pronounced Evangeline darkly. "She hates doctors. She tries to kill them. It's time to put her in an asylum, Andi!"

I lifted my gaze. Bianca's hair was the color of midnight, shot through with bands of cobalt. Her mouth was the color of ripe strawberries. Her nose was perfection itself. But her eyes! Dark as all eternity, brimming with a childlike wonder that was completely at odds with what I had seen within them earlier, for now it was like looking into the portals of heaven.

In comparison to Bianca, Clarissa and Daphne were ugly stepsisters.

Bianca reached out a shapely, trusting hand and laid it gently on my arm.

I trembled.

Andelucia's voice reeled me back from the brink. "Doctor," she said fervently, and there was something in her tone that suggested the storm weathered and a safe harbor reached, "you must lead a charmed life."

I choked on my spit.

11

"Charmed," I said.

I laughed the bitter laugh.

The irony of it was appalling.

Dinner was over and I was alone with Grandfather. He did not respond, of course.

"She obviously doesn't know me very well," I added darkly.

I meant Andelucia.

"And isn't it ironic," I said, "that the one girl who has ever looked at me in just the way I've always dreamed of being looked at should happen to be a complete idiot?"

I meant Bianca. Evangeline was right—there was something very, very wrong with Bianca—mainly that she had formed an inexplicable attachment to me.

Me!

A pariah.

A monkey's paw.

And that wasn't the only thing wrong with Bianca. She also hadn't said a single word throughout the course of the evening.

And her sisters—they acted as though nothing was out of the ordinary—as if Bianca's mute nakedness was as natural as the coming of springtime.

Ludicrous!

It had been a singularly unnerving evening.

I went to the window and stared at nothing.

"Also," I said harshly, "I'm not a doctor. I'm only here because Sebastian sent me to kill Andelucia. But I can't kill Andelucia. I can't kill anyone."

I stared out the window some more.

Darkness rose in the east, gently lacing the trees with threads of night.

"He'll expect to find her dead, of course. He'll expect to find her dead but she'll be alive, thanks to me. So I really have to go."

Bianca's alabaster perfection passed before the theater of my mind.

"And yet, I cannot leave," I mused. "If I leave, he'll just send someone else to do what I cannot."

A piece of moon climbed into the sky.

"So I can't leave."

I returned to Grandfather's bedside.

I picked up a small, ornate bottle sitting on the squat table beside the bed. Murky liquid swirled in its depths. Indecipherable instructions were pasted on the side of the bottle.

I put the bottle back down.

"He'll expect to find you alive, with your medications properly administered. He'll expect to find you alive, but you'll be dead, because the only thing I know about doctoring is chicken soup and peppermint tea. And the only reason I know about the soup and tea is because that's all I can remember of my mother."

Grandfather twitched, so I knew he was still alive.

"Charmed," I added bitterly.

I went to bed.

12

I did not sleep.

Thoughts and images whirled round and round in my brain while the stars shifted in their orbits.

The old house creaked fitfully, as if unknown persons were strolling across the boards, and the hair on the back of my neck stood on end.

Sebastian!

Of course, it couldn't be Sebastian. Not now. Not yet. But what with the darkness of the night and the strangeness of the room and the lateness of the hour, I was convinced it was he.

I stared into the darkness and willed the door not to open.

The door opened.

I lay there, paralyzed.

The figure that stood in the doorway, awash in moonlight, was not that of Sebastian.

It was Bianca.

My heart started beating again.

"Bianca!" I exclaimed in heartfelt tones. "Boy, am I glad to see you! I thought it was Sebastian coming for me!"

In my relief I had forgotten how uncomfortable it was to be in her presence.

Bianca's eyes sparkled, unnaturally bright, like stars fallen to earth, and her magic began to weave its spell once more. She said nothing, but flew across the room, a nymph drenched in moonlight, an effervescent creature lighter than air.

She snuggled into bed with me, curling up beside me and taking possession of my arm and staring up at me with eyes that smoked like autumn leaves.

The world swam before my eyes. From her hair rose the scent of fresh mulberries. Her bare hip, awash with moonlight, was a pool of fresh cream.

The air felt suddenly very thick.

Time stood still.

And then the house creaked some more and a figure entered the room, dark and menacing.

"Sebastian!" I screeched.

It wasn't Sebastian.

"Doctor?"

It was Andelucia, which was much, much worse. I quietly died a thousand deaths. I opened my mouth once or twice to protest my innocence, but no sound was forthcoming.

Bianca's grip on my arm tightened.

"Bianca!" Andelucia sounded exasperated. "Are you pestering the poor doctor?"

Bianca's lower lip quivered.

Andelucia sighed. "I'm so sorry, Doctor. I've been looking all over for her. She was inconsolable after you left, but I never dreamed she'd disturb you."

"I—she just came in," I said stupidly.

"You poor man," murmured Andelucia, and her words were tonic to the bruised and battered soul.

But then Andelucia quirked her brow. "Doctor," she said, and the very gentleness of her voice made my spine quiver. "Do you think she could stay here with you? Just for tonight, I mean."

I wabbled my mouth, but my vocal chords weren't paying attention.

Bianca nestled her head against my shoulder.

"Thank you so much, Doctor," said Andelucia, bestowing a pleasant smile upon the two of us. "We'll figure out what's to be done in the morning."

"No." The word forced itself out of me at last, tattered and threadbare.

But Andelucia had closed the door gently behind her.

I lay rigid in the bed. The exquisiteness that lay beside me relaxed. Her breathing became even and rhythmic. Her shoulder rose and fell gently in the moonlight. The warmth of her body seeped into mine.

My arm went to sleep.

I did not.

There would be no sleep for me that night.

The moon shifted in the night sky.

Shadows moved along the far wall.

I forced myself to breathe.

Turned my thoughts to other things.

Sebastian, for instance.

Sebastian—

I sat bolt upright in bed.

Bianca stirred and snuggled closer.

The thought which had exploded in my head was absolutely insane. But in the dead of night, in a world of darkness and shadows, it made perfect sense.

The thought ricocheted back and forth.

What if Sebastian never arrived?

13

I extricated my arm from Bianca's embrace.

Moonlight played upon her perfect features, a symphony in black and white, but she did not awaken. It seemed the most natural thing in the world to—

I bent over her sleeping form.

Her beauty filled the room—

Awkwardly, clumsily, I touched my lips to the coolness of her perfect brow.

Breathing hard, I slipped out of the whitewashed room and tiptoed through the somnolent house and out into the silvery night.

The air was cool and bracing. The quiet was intense, as though the world was holding its breath.

The barn sat lower on the hill, a behemoth cloaked in deep shadow, a dark blot upon a twinkling landscape.

My footsteps crunched along the gravel drive. I followed an overgrown sidetrack to the barn and entered a side door. I stepped into velvety darkness, stumbled over a pile of bricks, and banged into a harness.

A horse whinnied softly.

I stopped blundering around and waited until my eyes grew accustomed to the darkness.

On the far wall I found a workbench. Above it, buried in shadow, was a board weighted with tools. I selected a rugged handsaw and a pipe wrench that looked like they meant business.

I headed out into the night, filled with purpose and determination.

The bridge was a lot farther away than I remembered. Under the brittle light of the moon it also looked considerably larger. More formidable. It was a single vehicle wide and perhaps fifty feet in length, timbered and railed, but it spanned a gash in the land a good fifty feet deep.

A handsaw and a pipe wrench were completely inadequate for what I had in mind. A stash of dynamite, on the other hand, would have been an excellent start. What had seemed, in the comfort of my bed, a simple solution, now revealed itself to be patently impossible.

I could not destroy the bridge.

Sebastian would not be stopped.

Besides, if I took out the bridge, how would Andelucia get into town for necessities? True,

Evangeline's activity with the trowel indicated the possibility of a garden. And since Andelucia had just laid in a month's supply of groceries, starvation wouldn't be immediate; nevertheless, I found myself stymied.

I sighed the thin and colorless sigh and stepped out onto the bridge. Loose planks shifted beneath my feet. Wide openings between the warped boards gave me bleak glimpses of the dark gulf below. Rotting cross timbers groaned.

I understood Andelucia's concern for the bridge and wondered why it hadn't already collapsed under its own weight.

I proceeded across the bridge, no clear direction in my mind, and with only a vague understanding that if I continued walking I might eventually reach the train station.

I could not see beyond that, and even the station seemed a remote and intangible possibility. But putting one foot in front of the other was better than doing nothing.

Nearly midway across the bridge I paused.

The railing on one side had been compromised, and the splintered remnants of wood made it clear that a vehicle had gone over the edge.

I stepped closer, peering into the blackness below. A thin gurgle indicated the presence of a brook somewhere beneath me.

For want of something to do, I knelt and extended my arm through what was left of the splintered railing and attempted to wrestle a bolt loose with the pipe wrench. It didn't want to budge, so I applied more pressure. It was still no good, so I gritted my teeth and put my back into it—

The wrench slipped off the bolt and went whirling into space, catching flecks of moonlight as it disappeared into the abyss below. I nearly followed, but managed to catch myself with nothing worse than a moment of dizzying vertigo. A distant *thunk* served to mark the end of the wrench's journey. I shuddered and returned to the center of the bridge.

However, it had not escaped my notice that the crossbeam was new, possibly replaced as a result of the accident. I wondered if the solution to my dilemma was staring me in the face.

I bent down, thrusting the saw between two weather-beaten boards, and placed the teeth of the saw against the new timber.

I commenced humming an aimless tune in counterpoint to my sawing. The saw went through the wood like butter.

14

The moon was moving towards the horizon and blisters were rising and bursting on my hands and the butter had turned to stone before the beam parted.

In a way, the parting of the beam gave me a sense of something akin to triumph. Perhaps this was the way a knight in shining armor felt as he dashed to the rescue of the fair maiden.

Conquering.

Victorious.

Valorous.

I straightened and dashed the sweat from my brow in the split second preceding what sounded like rifle shots as the bridge broke in half.

I shut my eyes and waited for the bridge to collapse. The bridge swayed like a drunken man, timbers groaning, but did not immediately fall down, so I opened my eyes and moved cautiously towards solid ground.

And then I stopped dead in my tracks.

There was a figure standing at the edge of the bridge, a smudge of black on black.

My mouth went dry and my hands became clammy. My heart banged against my ribs.

Sebastian!

How he had crossed the bridge without my knowing I could not tell, but there he stood, a hulking, menacing figure with fire in his eyes. I took a firmer grip on the saw and wished that I still had the pipe wrench.

The sky in the east shifted from black to gray.

"Bianca!" I yelled.

The hulking figure morphed into an ivory angel, a naked sculpture in white marble, and for a long moment I drank from the fountain of her exquisite beauty.

I scowled. "What's so funny?"

Bianca's shoulders were heaving, as though convulsed in laughter.

She was not laughing.

She was sobbing, great tears welling out of luminous eyes and spilling down her porcelain cheeks; she cried as though her heart was breaking.

"Bianca!" I cried, closing the distance between us in a mad sprint, unmindful of the bridge wobbling beneath me like a giant slab of gelatin.

The moment I set foot on solid ground Bianca flung

herself at me—knocking the saw out of my grasp, such was the force of her exuberance—and wrapping me in an embrace that spoke of a desperation beyond my comprehension.

A girl.

In my arms.

Soft and inviting and—

I stood there awkwardly.

A low sound of contentment came from Bianca. She lifted radiant eyes to mine, and her eyes were like midnight jewels. Her smile, warm and adoring, went straight to my heart, and my arms, of their own accord, rose to return her embrace—

"You're freezing!" I blurted, finding refuge in the mundane. "Here, take my shirt." And suiting action to words, I disengaged myself from her embrace and fumbled with the buttons of my shirt, removing it hastily and wrapping it snugly about her. "There!" I said, trying to steady my breathing. "You'll feel better in no time!"

I drew one or two self-composing breaths and hoped that I, too, would be feeling better in no time—

"You okay?" I queried.

Bianca's eyes had gone wide, and her expression had become one of unspeakable terror.

I shot a glance over my shoulder, fully expecting to see Sebastian. I saw no one; indeed, the bridge was motionless.

And yet, the horror within her grew; she trembled violently, uncontrollably. Worse, her eyes never left mine—they seemed to be begging me to release her from some nameless agony.

"What is it?" I prompted, but she trembled all the more, and I feared convulsions would surely follow. "Speak to me! What's wrong?"

A thought, random and without foundation, came to me. "It's not—it can't be my shirt—can it?" My voice crescendoed into nothingness. It seemed that it could not be, that it had no relevance; nevertheless, I removed the garment from her.

The trembling subsided at once, the torment bled away from her eyes; her expression became once again one of rapt adoration.

"Of all the doggoned things," I muttered. I perceived there was more to her idiocy than met the eye.

Again she wrapped me in her arms, and the scent of mulberries enveloped me—

"No!" I yelped, startling her with the strength of my retreat, the caress of her skin against mine burning holes into my brain. Breathing hard, and trembling with a madness of my own, I shoved my arms into my shirt and buttoned it savagely. I retrieved the saw. "Let's go home," I muttered.

She took possession of my free arm, and her smile was one of perfect contentment.

We strolled into the dawn.

15

Sunrise was an orchestra of light and color. Birdsong fell from the treetops like bright confetti, scrubby woodland flowers waved to and fro, and the smell of pines poured a rich perfume over the world.

I forgot how exhausted I was.

I felt, incongruously, euphoric.

Almost, it was as if the bad luck that had plagued me my whole life had shifted—as if, by the simple act of taking a little initiative, I had broken the curse that had bound me for so long.

I sensed a new and wonderful destiny unfolding before me.

We reached the house—

"Good morning, Doctor!"

It was Andelucia, looking as fresh as the morning, and the breath caught in my throat. It was like I was seeing her again for the very first time. And in that moment

I experienced something of an epiphany—whereas Daphne and Clarissa and Bianca quickened the pulse, Andelucia quickened the soul. Her smile, the warmth in her eyes, her acknowledgment of me as a person—looking at her was like coming home.

Andelucia shook her head wonderingly. "Bianca is a different girl altogether now that you're here, Doctor," she said. "We're so lucky to have you."

Lucky.

Luck had obviously repented of her misdeeds and was doing her level best to make amends. Luck was fawning over me as a mother fawns over a new child.

"And don't let Clarissa forget her tryst with Frederick," Andelucia was saying as she climbed into her car.

"I won't," I said huskily. Probably I had known from the start what Andelucia meant to me; certainly, I had known before our ride home was over. There was a connection between us that I couldn't put into words. Probably it had been this bond that had stopped my hand when it was within my power to fulfill Sebastian's instructions.

But now—now I would tell her everything, and maybe—well, maybe the telling of it would take a lifetime.

Andelucia reached her hand out of the car window and touched my arm. "Your breakfast is on the table," she said, and my throat constricted and my cup of happiness spilled over. She started the car, gave me another radiant smile, and with a spitting of gravel, drove off.

16

I was still waving farewell when the door to the house banged open and Evangeline appeared. She was still in her nightgown, a faded garment that fell to her ankles, severe at the throat and sleeves and hem. Her ruddy hair was mussed and she was scowling.

"Leggo of her!" she snarled, wresting Bianca away from me. She gave me a penetrating glare. "Your shirt's buttoned wrong, you pervert," she added nastily.

I gave Evangeline a tender smile. In my elevated mood I could not be touched even by the likes of her.

Bianca reached for me with the look of one who does not understand why the best thing in her world is being denied her.

"Stop it, Bianca!" snapped Evangeline. She glared at me. "What are you doing with Sebastian's saw?" She yanked the saw out of my hand. "What are you up to, Doctor?"

She placed special emphasis on the title, as though to mock it.

"Saving lives," I murmured, having my little joke.

"Where's Andelucia?" she demanded. "Has she already gone?"

"Gone?" I said.

"She has gone!" wailed Evangeline. "I was going to remind her to check the mail!"

"Gone," I said. "No. Andelucia only goes into town once a month. She told me so herself. She only goes into town once a month to do her shopping, and yesterday was that day so she can't be going into town, not for another month. Besides, Sebastian is coming here first. I'm the new doctor, and Sebastian is coming to check on me. She said so. So no, to answer your question, no. No, she hasn't gone."

It seemed imperative that I make Evangeline understand.

Evangeline glared at me. "This is all your fault," she said accusingly. "We can't afford butter, but she's going off to town to buy you some clothes because you didn't bring any with you." She gave me a scornful look. "She says you slept in your clothes last night. Doctor, my foot!"

"But the bridge." My voice was a yellow trickle of sound. "She'll be killed. The bridge isn't safe. She'll die and be killed and she'll die."

Evangeline looked at me shrewdly. "I'm keeping my eye on you, buster," she warned, turning on her heel and dragging a reluctant Bianca into the house.

17

"Andelucia is dead," I informed Grandfather brutally.

Time had, unbelievably, continued its relentless march. At first I had wandered aimlessly through the house.

Numb.

In shock.

Confession, they say, is good for the soul—

"I killed her," I told him. "I sabotaged the bridge and I killed her. Me. I couldn't have killed her better if I had tried."

I forced Grandfather into a sitting position. He was nearly comatose, but I persevered and managed to get a little chicken soup into him. In my wanderings I had spent some time in the kitchen. Considerable time. "Ironic, really. When I was trying to kill her, I couldn't. And when I thought I was saving her, I wasn't. Maybe it is fate. More than likely, it's just my rotten luck. Call it what you will, it sure pulled out all the stops this time.

"On the bright side," I added, chuckling without mirth, "I'm no longer in debt to Sebastian."

Grandfather drooled on himself.

I hardened my voice. "I guess what I'm trying to say is that Andelucia isn't going to be taking care of you anymore. Neither is Clarissa, because she's marrying Frederick. Ironic, really—two souls embarking on a new life together, while another two souls follow Andelucia into the eternities.

"And as for Daphne and Evangeline—" I continued, "well, you can just imagine how well they'd take care of you!"

I gave him a sip of peppermint tea. Then I patted his back until he could breathe again. "I'm not enjoying this either," I informed him. "But even a condemned man deserves a last meal." I shook my head and made an observation. "You, sir, are a mess." I removed his nightshirt.

And then, because the smells coming from him seemed to warrant it, I removed the rest of his clothing.

"If it makes you feel any better," I said, trying not to breathe as I bathed him with a washcloth and some soap from a bucket of warm water, "you'll never have to go through this again."

I lotioned some ugly bedsores with some ointment

from his bedside. Perhaps I was only postponing the inevitable, but I also changed his bedding.

"I'm not even sure why I'm doing this," I said bitterly. "Unless it's to honor Andelucia's memory. See, for a moment I thought perhaps there might be a chance—"

I drew the curtain on the thought, went to the closet and returned with a pair of black trousers, a white shirt, and a black bow tie, which seemed somehow appropriate. I dressed him while he slept, then got down to business.

Grandfather's medicines covered the dresser and bedside table and bookcase. A number of them sported skulls and crossbones and included dire warnings regarding doses. It was apparent that the previous twelve doctors had all left rather abruptly. Fortunately, they had left behind an apothecary's dream.

Or nightmare, depending on your point of view.

"In the wrong hands," I said, having my little joke, "these things could kill someone."

I dumped the medicines and tinctures and tonics into an empty beaker. I crushed the pills and tablets into powder with a mortar and pestle, then added them to the mixture.

I stirred the concoction.

The aroma was noxious and made my eyes water.

With bitter eyes I looked at the sunlight pouring through the windows, making bright mockery of

Andelucia's death.

I set my jaw.

To have found the girl of my dreams.

To have killed her, however unwittingly.

Luck.

I was going to steal Luck's thunder.

"Bottoms up," I said, and without further ceremony tipped the entirety of Grandfather's medicines into my mouth.

I swallowed. Twice. Three times.

And then I kept swallowing in order to keep the stuff down.

Tears sprang to my eyes.

I staggered into the chair at Grandfather's bedside. My gaze went to the door to his room. Lingered there.

The door did not open.

Apparently, when Evangeline put her mind to it, Bianca could not wander free.

"See you on the other side," I told Grandfather tonelessly, "which will be soon enough."

The sense of—

A song—

My stomach lurched and I closed my eyes.

18

"Doctor?"

I was wakened by a gentle hand upon my shoulder.

"I'm sorry to disturb you—you looked so peaceful."

I blinked open my eyes, confused and disoriented. Sunlight no longer poured through the windows. Shadows had shifted, and there was the hint of pine and sage in the air. I had the sensation of the passage of time.

"She wasn't always this way, you know,"Andelucia continued. "Before the accident she was as normal as you or me. Afterwards—well, you see how it is."

I didn't see a thing. I tried to pierce the fog surrounding my disorientation.

"Before your arrival she tried to kill every man she set eyes on. I think it must have been your smile. When you smiled at her she put down the gun. You have a very engaging smile, Doctor."

My body felt stiff and awkward; my muscles seemed

to have atrophied.

"Sebastian had to move out," continued Andelucia. "Bianca went after Frederick with a poker. The twelve doctors before you barely escaped with their lives. Of course, Evangeline is partly to blame—she is forever letting Bianca out of her room."

Bianca was sitting on the floor, her head on my knee, her exquisite legs curled beneath her. She was holding my hand. I caught a whiff of mulberry.

"She didn't keep you awake last night, did she?" Andelucia asked anxiously.

I drank in the wonder of Andelucia, the curve of her cheek, the depths of her hazel eyes, the hair curling at her neck, the hollow of her throat. And in that moment she was more beautiful than Bianca could ever hope to be.

Her hand lingered on my shoulder.

"You're alive," I said. The words were lumpy and coarse. My mouth was dry and my tongue wooden. Bianca stirred at the sound of my voice, lifting her head to smile at me, the fold of my trousers imprinted upon her cheek.

Andelucia chuckled. "Funny you should say that. I think another one of the bridge timbers gave way on my way back. The county really needs to get busy and repair that thing before it kills somebody." She shifted her gaze to look at Bianca. "You know, I feel I can breathe again, now you're here."

I moved my hand. "I'm not dead," I said.

Andelucia laughed. "And neither is Grandfather. You've taken better care of him than the last dozen doctors all put together." She squeezed my shoulder. "We're so lucky to have you."

My eyes could not look at her enough.

She looked back, and her slow, sweet smile made me wonder if she was thinking the same thing that I was thinking. Fate had brought us together and Fate, it appeared, was not going to be thwarted.

"Dinner is ready," said Andelucia.

"That's just how I feel," I said thickly.

Andelucia quirked her brow. "Excuse me?"

"Nothing," I said. "I—nothing!"

And then I lurched to my feet, dislodging Bianca and startling Andelucia, who quickly withdrew her hand. I swayed uncertainly before bolting. "Bathroom," I croaked.

I made haste.

19

Evangeline glared at Andelucia. "How could you forget?" she demanded. Her hair still wasn't combed, but she had changed her pajamas for the inevitable pair of overalls.

"I had other things on my mind," said Andelucia placatingly.

"I just *knew* you would forget!" wailed Evangeline.

Andelucia had failed to check the mail.

Daphne giggled.

Evangeline whirled on her. "What's so funny about it? I *need* those seeds!"

Daphne regarded her blankly. "What? Oh. That. No. I was thinking of something else. I was thinking of ol' Fishface proposing to Clarissa. I was thinking—will she have to kiss him, do you think?"

Evangeline gave a snort of disgust.

I felt like a new man. The nap had done me a world

of good, and I found, after my discomfiture in the bathroom, that I was starving. I drew a deep and glorious breath.

Daphne lifted her eyes. "When the man of my dreams proposes to me, I'll bet he crushes me in his arms and showers my brow with kisses."

I reached across my plate for my silverware. My right arm had been appropriated by Bianca. Occasionally she nibbled food from my plate, but mostly she just watched me with an expression of puppy-like devotion.

"I'll bet the man of my dreams tells me his life is naught but a hollow shell without me. After he showers my brow with kisses, I mean."

"Gah!" said Evangeline.

"Eat your food, Daphne," suggested Andelucia dryly.

There came the sound of chimes.

Evangeline jumped.

"I should think I would rather like my brow to be showered with kisses," added Daphne wistfully.

"Somebody's at the door," said Evangeline.

"Don't be a goof, Evangeline." Daphne rolled her eyes. "No one calls here. Ever." There was a trace of bitterness in her voice. "Because of Bianca."

Andelucia caught my eye. "Sometimes the wind comes in through the library window and the chimes—"

The chimes sounded again, imperatively.

Andelucia broke off, frowning. "Perhaps you'd better go check, Daphne. We'll keep an eye on Bianca."

"I'm right in the middle of my marriage proposal!" Daphne complained, but she pushed back her chair and went to check.

Andelucia cast a troubled glance out the window. "Speaking of Clarissa, she should be getting back soon."

"What are you grinning about?" Evangeline burst out fiercely.

She was addressing me.

"Evangeline!" said Andelucia sharply. "That is no way to address the doctor!"

I hadn't been aware that I was grinning. I had only been thinking how nice it was that instead of discussing Andelucia's death, the conversation was revolving around the innocuous and mundane.

Nevertheless, in deference to Evangeline, I undid my smile. "I was just thinking that Andelucia was right," I told her gravely. "I think maybe I *do* lead a charmed life."

Strong words indeed, coming from one who had, until recently, perceived himself as the unluckiest person in the world. However, I could not escape the feeling that everything had happened for the best and could only get better.

The scathing retort hovering on Evangeline's lips was destined never to be uttered, for at that moment

Daphne swept impressively back into the room.

"It's Fishface!" she burst out, pausing only long enough to ensure that she had our undivided attention before continuing in swelling tones, "He says it's Clarissa! He says there's been an accident! He says to bring the doctor and to *hurry!*"

20

I held on to the handle of the black bag as Andelucia guided Daisy down an embankment and into a ravine. The pony cart's springs groaned as the wheels jolted against the stony ground. Daisy did not seem to understand the need for speed, but ambled along at a leisurely pace.

The bag was empty, of course, but Andelucia had requested I bring it along. She could have requested I turn hand springs and I would have made the attempt.

Daphne and Evangeline and Frederick had gone on ahead on foot by way of the road. Bianca had been confined to her room.

Apparently, Luck was being unexpectedly generous.

I was referring, of course, to Clarissa's accident. Her accident provided me with time alone with Andelucia, and time alone with Andelucia was what I particularly desired. "Earlier," I said, "I thought maybe I heard you say something about my—well, about my smile. Earlier, that is. I was still a little groggy so I guess I could have been mistaken but it sounded like you said it was—well, I was just wondering what it was you *had* said, in case I was mistaken."

The words, carefully rehearsed, nevertheless failed to come out as offhanded as I would have liked, and the sound of my inquiry hung clumsily in the air.

Nevertheless, I smiled engagingly and risked a glance at Andelucia.

She was staring straight ahead and her expression was troubled. "I'm worried about Clarissa, Doctor," she said pensively. "You see, she may see this accident as another omen and decide not to marry Frederick after all. I guess I'm partly to blame, since I'm always telling the girls that everything happens for a reason and there's a reason for everything that happens—but what they don't seem to fully grasp is that sometimes things happen to test our willingness to persevere in the face of adversity."

Shadows lengthened and birds flung their evening songs upon the air. A trickle of water accompanied us along the floor of the ravine.

"In Grandfather's room, I mean," I said. "I was just wondering if maybe I had heard you correctly, or if—well, if maybe I hadn't."

Andelucia's expression became even more pensive.

"If something should happen to prevent Clarissa from marrying Frederick—well, I just don't know what we'll do."

The walls of the ravine climbed into the sky, becoming less vegetative, more craggy, rugged.

The silence became oppressive.

"I—it's a beautiful evening," I said weakly.

Andelucia gave me a strange look.

I tightened my grip on the black bag.

And then the smile which I knew I would never tire of appeared and Andelucia laid a warm hand on my arm. "Thank you, Doctor," she said. "You are absolutely right, of course. Clarissa will marry Frederick. There will be money enough. Everything will turn out just as it should. You see, it's just that sometimes it seems that the things we wish for so often come to naught. Still, instead of borrowing trouble, I could just as easily look on the bright side, and so—just as you say, Doctor—it *is* a beautiful evening."

I nodded dumbly.

We rounded a bend in the ravine.

Before us was an oddly frozen tableau. Frederick, Daphne and Evangeline, faces drawn, expressions stricken, stood over Clarissa. Clarissa's body was oddly twisted, and her gown was in unseemly disarray.

"Andi!" cried Daphne, starting forward. "Oh, Andi! I think she's—!"

"She's not *either!*" cried Evangeline sharply, moving closer to Frederick. "Don't say it, because she's not! She's *not!*"

Frederick was a slight figure with unkempt hair and a face reminiscent of a trout. He looked like he was trying unsuccessfully to recover from a blow and would be toppling over presently.

Next to Clarissa was a crossbeam, apparently recently cut, still bolted to a rotting length of timber. Above us, casting sharply angled shadows on the ravine wall, was the bridge.

21

Evangeline was absolutely right, of course. Clarissa wasn't dead. She couldn't be dead. Andelucia was counting on her to marry Frederick so she wasn't dead. Injured, certainly—but not dead. If she was dead it would ruin everything.

Nevertheless, a slender thread of ice wrapped itself around my spine.

"Of course she's not dead," said Andelucia, echoing my sentiments perfectly, and I breathed a little easier. Her manner, as she dropped the reins and leaped to the ground, was cheerfully reassuring.

I joined Andelucia as she bent over Clarissa and was relieved to see that Clarissa didn't look nearly as bad as I had first supposed. There was a copious amount of blood at her temple, which was a little scary. Blood matted her ice-blonde hair and pooled on the ground, but her head hardly looked bashed in at all.

Probably she was only resting.

Andelucia took Clarissa's wrist in her hand. Presently, she felt Clarissa's neck. Finally, she placed her ear against Clarissa's bosom.

Daphne and Evangeline and Frederick drew closer.

Then, very slowly, very deliberately, Andelucia folded Clarissa's arms upon her chest. She turned to me, and although her eyes were clear, there was a peculiar catch in her voice.

"She's dead, Doctor."

22

The world swam before my eyes.

Andelucia rose abruptly. "Doctor! Are you okay?"

I fought to maintain my balance. The thread had become a chain, and the chain was wrapped around my throat. "Maybe she's—resting."

A soft smile appeared on Andelucia's strained countenance. "Oh, Doctor! It's not your fault. She was dead when we got here. There was nothing you could have done. I'm sure she died instantly, which is a mercy. Are you sure you're okay?"

An abyss had opened up beneath me, black as death and stretching into all eternity. I was falling—falling—

Evangeline was suddenly before me, pummeling my chest with balled-up fists, her face ashen. "*Do* something, Doctor!" she screamed. "She wasn't supposed to *die!* You can't let her *die!* She *can't* die! *Do* something!"

I clung to her as a drowning man clings to a reed.

The staccato rhythm of her fists ceased; still clenching her fists against my chest, she folded herself into my arms.

Evangeline.

It would have been disconcerting had I been capable of rational thought.

"It was the beam." Frederick was speaking, and his voice had a wistful quality about it, as though the reality of the situation lay just beyond his grasp. "It came loose just as you were driving over, Andelucia—it struck her just as I was—she was standing just about there, or maybe there, and then the beam came down—it almost missed her, but then it didn't, and she—" His voice faded and his expression became introspective.

Daphne burst into sobs, her arms hanging uselessly by her sides, the tears raw and ragged, coming in tortured gusts.

"I killed her," I said dully, and the sound of my voice reached me as though from a great distance. "It was my fault. The bridge. The beam. I killed her."

Evangeline stiffened in my arms, and then she snuggled closer, her head tucked into the hollow of my throat, her coppery hair tickling my chin, her fists close to my heart.

Daphne's tears continued unabated.

"Don't be silly, Doctor," said Andelucia firmly. "You needed clothes. It wasn't your fault. We may not understand the reason, but you can rest assured there is a plan—a grand design—even in this. Besides, if we're going to start pointing fingers we might as well start with the county for not having fixed this bridge ages ago."

"She asked me if I thought I might break my legs someday—quite by accident, of course," said Frederick distantly. "I—the bridge—"

"You don't understand," I tried again, the sound of my voice cracked and grating. "I killed her. The bridge. The beam. You see, I—"

"That will be enough, Doctor." The words were a gentle rebuke.

I closed my mouth.

Andelucia went to Frederick and spoke a few low words to him. He shook his head; she spoke again, more urgently, and presently he nodded vaguely. Mumbling something about the bridge he turned and meandered away, following the floor of the ravine around a bend and out of sight.

Andelucia watched him go before returning to us. She seemed to have aged somewhat. She placed a hand on Evangeline's shoulder and Evangeline reluctantly removed herself from my embrace.

"Doctor?"

I looked at Andelucia hopelessly, but she didn't seem to notice. Presently I went to my knees and slipped a hand beneath Clarissa's shoulders, the other beneath the folds of her gown. Grunting a bit, I lifted her into my arms; her head lolled awkwardly. She was heavier than I would have guessed; nevertheless, and swaying a bit, I staggered over to the pony cart. There was something oddly intimate in my cradling of her—as though, in another time, in another place, she might have been carried thusly over a threshold.

It was an intimacy I neither asked for nor desired.

I set her gently down on the bed of the cart.

23

I stood there a moment, staring at the loveliness that had once been Clarissa, at a life ended before its time—at hopes and dreams and desires cut disastrously short.

"Everything is ruined," I said dully.

"No," said Andelucia slowly. "Changed, perhaps—but we've endured change before. It's not ruined—just different. We'll pull through, Doctor—you'll see. It's not the end of the world. The sun will shine again."

She was wrong, of course.

Dead wrong.

It was the end of the world.

"Where—what are we going to do with her?" Evangeline wanted to know.

"Although I sure didn't see this particular change coming," admitted Andelucia. She turned to Evangeline. "We'll take her to be with Grandmother, of course."

Daphne sobbed the more.

Evangeline latched onto my hand. "Not the crypt—you can't take her to the *crypt!* It's all *wrong!*"

Andelucia smiled gently. "We can't put her in her room, can we?"

"Bianca." Evangeline's voice was small and unsubstantial.

"Exactly. And the barn's out, of course."

"Daisy," said Evangeline brokenly.

"And we really can't leave her here, can we?"

"But we'll never see her again!" The pressure on my hand was a vice.

"She'll be waiting for us," said Andelucia soothingly, "on the other side. Just like Mother and Father and Grandmother and—"

Evangeline raised anguished eyes to mine. "This is the worst day in the world!"

Daphne's tears reached epic proportions.

Andelucia and I boarded the pony cart, leaving Daphne and Evangeline to walk home, the one still bawling, the other staring after us with empty eyes.

The mausoleum was located a mile or so beyond the house, set into the side of a wooded bluff that rose from the floor of the ravine. The building was a gloomy edifice of brick and marble, echoing in both style and substance the house.

"Grandfather and Grandmother built the house and crypt when they were young," explained Andelucia, seemingly disinclined to proceed with the task at hand. "Brick by brick, stone by stone. Of course, there was money in those days. Lots of money. Mother and Father spent it like water."

The sun touched the horizon, staining the sky with blood.

"But then the ship Mother and Father were on went down as they were sailing home from Europe. Sebastian blamed it on luck. They were supposed to have sailed a week earlier. It wasn't luck, of course—it was their destiny." She stared into the distance, a bemused expression on her face. "We had a dreadful row over it, but it wasn't really about luck or destiny—it was just our way of reacting to their deaths."

I watched the shadows lengthen, and sometimes I heard what she was saying, and sometimes her words were lost in the fog that filled my mind.

"I guess we believed the bankroll was inexhaustible—but the bank accounts yielded little. We sold some furniture. All the real jewelry. The servants had to go....

"And then—the accident with Bianca. Grandfather's sudden illness. And now—"

I twitched.

An uncomfortable moment passed.

"She liked fine things, Doctor. Of course, hearing

them talk you would think it was Daphne who liked the things that money can buy, but it was really Clarissa. Daphne is the practical one—Clarissa was the dreamer. Gowns. Jewelry. Shoes. I wish now that I had saved a piece of real jewelry for her."

Andelucia turned clouded eyes to me, and there was desolation in her voice. "Doctor—whatever will I do?"

I stared at her as one stares at a stranger.

"Sebastian," I said hollowly.

Sebastian was going to kill me. When he found out I had killed the wrong girl he was going to tear me apart with his bare hands. He had sent me to perform a simple task—I had botched it. He was going to slaughter me.

Andelucia nodded slowly. "You're right, of course, Doctor—Sebastian will know just exactly what to do. We'll leave poor Clarissa here for now and when Sebastian arrives we'll have a proper interment." She tendered me a tremulous smile and reached out her hand to touch my arm with her fingertips. "Whatever would we do without you, Doctor?"

I shuddered.

Andelucia alighted. The steps cut into the rock leading to the mausoleum were steep and eternal. I collected Clarissa and commenced climbing. The weight of Clarissa in my arms was as nothing compared to the weight upon my soul. I observed the lines of Clarissa's throat, the hair falling like a silvery river, the noble brow—ironic, really, that she should look so alive in death, so vibrant.

Andelucia opened the door for me and I laid Clarissa on a concrete slab in the center of the room, puffing somewhat. The air inside the mausoleum was cool; brown and withered leaves moved dismally in odd corners. Andelucia tenderly arranged Clarissa's gown. She stroked the ice-blonde hair on the side of Clarissa's head that wasn't damaged. She looked at her a long moment.

Then she bent and bestowed a tender kiss upon her brow.

"Goodbye for now, sister dear," she said softly.

I rubbed feeling back into my arms.

24

I stared into the depths of my soup, trying to find meaning in the wreckage that my arrival had precipitated. Better that I had been the cause of Andelucia's death than to have brought such tragedy into her life.

Well, no—I certainly wouldn't want that.

Better that I had not met Sebastian.

Except then I wouldn't have met Andelucia, and I wouldn't want that either.

Better had I never been born.

Bianca was not in evidence.

Evangeline, however, had taken possession of Bianca's chair and was hanging onto my hand for dear life.

Ironic.

Andelucia broke the silence. "I've asked Frederick to drop by in the morning."

Daphne looked up quickly. Her blue eyes were still dimmed by tears, but now there appeared in them an odd mixture of defiance and despair. "I am not going to marry Fishface!"

A thoughtful frown creased Andelucia's brow. "It cannot be coincidence that Frederick should be forced to marry just when we stand on the brink of financial ruin."

"I've made no secret of my dislike for him!" wailed Daphne.

"'Brick by brick, stone by stone, we built this place. Never sell it.' That's what Grandmother said—her very words." Andelucia smiled briefly. "Of course, if Sebastian had his way the house and land would be sold post-haste. I guess that's why the property was left to me. I promised Grandmother we'd never sell."

"He looks like a fish!" sobbed Daphne. "Like a—a trout!"

"Besides," continued Andelucia musingly, "Sebastian has already helped out more than we can ever hope to repay by taking care of Grandfather's medical bills. We've sold all the heirlooms with any real value—Frederick really is our only hope."

"Sell the Packard!" said Daphne fiercely. "We can sell the Packard and pay the taxes and still have enough left over for butter, and maybe a new sash."

Andelucia smiled her soft smile. "Well, I suppose it might help temporarily. But, of course, the Packard belongs to Sebastian. It's not ours to sell."

"I don't *care!*" cried Daphne. "I *won't* marry Fishface! When I get married, my husband is going to shower my brow with kisses. I can't let a—a *trout*—shower my brow with kisses! Make Evangeline marry him!"

The pressure on my hand intensified.

Andelucia slowly shook her head. "There's no need to get worked up about it, Daphne—you see, *I* am going to marry Frederick. Not you."

Stunned silence greeted this pronouncement and the room tilted dangerously.

"But—but you *can't* marry him!" cried Daphne, evincing an attitude completely at odds with the one previously expressed, but in complete accord with the thoughts clamoring for attention in my own head. "What about Grandfather? What about Bianca? What about me and Evangeline and Daisy and—and the doctor? You simply *can't* marry him!"

Andelucia's laughter sounded a little shaky. "Actually, my dear, I don't seem to have much of a choice in the matter. Besides," she continued distantly, "if I hadn't encouraged Clarissa to marry Frederick she'd be alive today—yes, Doctor?"

"Nothing," I said hoarsely.

"This is all *wrong!*" cried Daphne, and her tears commenced falling again, spilling from blue eyes into her soup.

"In truth, it's not what I would have chosen either," said Andelucia soberly. And then, striving for a brighter tone, she turned to me. "Doctor, you haven't touched your food."

"I—I'm not hungry."

Her expression softened. "I understand."

She didn't understand.

She couldn't understand.

Never in a million years would she—

"I miss Clarissa," said Evangeline in a small voice. She brought my hand to her chest, hugged it tightly.

Andelucia favored me with a tender look. "Doctor," she said softly, "you are such a comfort."

I yanked my hand free, rose abruptly and fled the room.

25

"I killed Clarissa!" I shouted at Grandfather. "Me! I did it! It was all my fault! I *murdered* her!"

He did not respond.

I laughed raucously. "She was to have been engaged—she was to have been *married!*"

My hands were shaking so badly that Grandfather ended up wearing most of the chicken soup I was trying to feed him.

"Luck!" I bellowed, trying to shout a reaction out of him. "Andelucia can spout homilies about plans and designs and some higher purpose, but I know better—boy, do I ever know better! Luck holds the trump card and there's not a thing you or I or anyone else can do about it!"

The irony of it all was killing me—or, to be more precise, it was killing Clarissa—*had* killed her.

Peppermint tea he didn't want went down Grandfather's throat. He may have made noises of protest, but I ignored them.

My course was abundantly clear. There would be no shilly-shallying around with tinctures and tonics this time.

This time I would not be stopped.

I bathed and changed Grandfather a last time, roughly, without ceremony, then banged into my room with the black bag to collect the only things that mattered.

I was referring to my new clothes, of course. The clothes that Andelucia had purchased for me at the cost of Clarissa's life. They meant more to me than she would ever know. She had sacrificed money she didn't have—on me. It had seemed to portend better things, a brighter day.

A day that was not to be.

The light bleeding from the sky cast my room into gloom so I did not immediately perceive that my room was already occupied.

And then the blood froze in my veins.

"Sebastian!" I yelled, shaking so badly that the black bag fell to the floor.

It was Bianca, of course. She rose from my bed, a cool flame ascending, a naked goddess unfolding, to greet me. Her lips were parted in happy anticipation, and the liquid depths of her eyes gave me to understand that I was the best and brightest thing in her world.

"What's wrong with you!" I yelled at her. "I just killed your sister! Get away from me before I kill you too!"

She flinched, as though struck.

"I am going to rid the world of my pestilent presence once and for all!" I bellowed.

She reached hesitantly for me, her expression a curious mixture of bewilderment and desire. The rising moon touched her skin, rendering it hauntingly poetic.

I grabbed her fiercely by the shoulders. "You complete and abysmal idiot!" I shouted savagely, shaking her furiously.

She melted into my arms.

I shook deep within my soul. "What am I going to do with you?"

She clung to me like a shadow.

We stood together a long moment, and as we lingered the texture of the night deepened.

At length, I guided her to the bed.

She did not want to be parted from me.

My plan would *not* be thwarted.

Delayed, perhaps—but not thwarted.

I joined her and she snuggled close. Her eyes were deep and inviting. It seemed the most natural thing in the world to return her embrace. Her breath was warm and sweet, her skin soft and tantalizing. Moonlight danced on the rippling contours of her shoulders, the small of her back, the swelling of her—

"Flesh and blood," I muttered, "can only take so much. Besides, Luck owes me this much—"

She moved her body against mine, making little animal noises of pleasure, and the weight of her body was intoxicating. I caressed the line of her cheek, touched the curve of her chin. Her mouth reached hungrily for mine, and billowing waves of adoration spilled from the warm depths of her dark eyes.

Adoration.

Mingled with trust.

Implicit, unfailing trust.

I—

I thrust her violently from me, leaping from the bed and finding the floor beneath my feet. "Get away from me!" I yelled, shaking uncontrollably.

She stared at me, confusion in her soft eyes. Moonlight drenched her as rain drenches a meadow. She reached out a tentative hand, a gesture that was at once simple and charming. A timid smile touched the corners of her mouth.

"Are you crazy?" I bellowed. "I can't—you shouldn't—what would your sister say?"

Her breasts cast eloquent shadows on her belly. Strands of midnight curled at her throat.

"Like trying to talk to Grandfather," I groaned. "You are *such* an idiot!"

She reached for me once more.

"No!" I shouted at her. "No, no, *no!* Don't you get it? A thousand times no! Don't you understand *anything? No!*"

Tears gathered in her eyes and spilled down her cheeks, glistening like jewels.

"Oh, stop your blubbering!" I snapped.

She turned away from me and curled herself into a tight ball.

"You're all insane!" I raved. "It's like I'm in an asylum, and you—you're the worst of the lot!"

Her shoulders trembled.

I glared at her bare backside.

Presently, I sighed.

"Oh, stop your crying," I muttered. "It was my fault—not yours. You didn't mean anything by it. It's me—I should have known better."

She sobbed as though her heart would break.

I came close and touched her alabaster shoulder. "Bianca," I said softly.

She jerked away from me and it was a knife twist to the soul.

And I saw, in that clarifying moment, that in preserving her virtue I had destroyed something else—something just as precious. I had tossed aside the opportunity of a lifetime and gained absolutely nothing in return.

"I am such an idiot," I said harshly.

I watched as Bianca cried herself to sleep.

26

I awoke to the sound of birds greeting the gray twilight of morning with song.

Stiff.

Sore.

Wondering where in the world I was.

I was on the floor, and the floor was hard and unforgiving.

I lumbered to my feet, stubbed my toe on the dresser and steadied myself on the bed.

Bianca stirred.

I froze.

She was exquisite in slumber. The lashes upon her cheek, the shape of her nose, the curve of her lips—too late I suffered an epiphany: what I felt for her wasn't the passion of a lover, nor was it the desire of a suitor. This went deeper somehow—and it was compounded by the gut-wrenching knowledge that I had ruined it forever.

I took the liberty of brushing a strand of glossy hair away from her face. "Goodbye forever," I murmured, before turning abruptly away.

I slipped noiselessly out of the room.

Out of the house.

The sky was buried in clouds.

I swung wide the great doors of the barn.

Andelucia's roadster was there—small, compact, lightweight.

So was Sebastian's Packard—over two tons of ebony metal and dull chrome, a dark, brooding beast lurking in the shadows.

With any luck, it would go through the bridge like a hot knife through butter.

But I did not trust Luck. Luck had played me for the fool too many times to be trusted.

I opened the trunk of the Packard. It wasn't spacious, but it would be more than adequate.

I commenced lugging bricks from the pile I had stumbled over on my last visit to the barn and stacked them in the trunk.

A wheelbarrow would have made the task easier, but I wasn't going to waste time scouting one up. Besides, frustration with life and luck was coursing through my veins like fuel and I felt like I had the strength of ten men.

I thought of Bianca.

I thought of her waking to find me gone.

I wondered if she would ever forgive me.

Or if she would even remember me.

I hesitated.

I thought of Evangeline.

Who was going to hold her hand when I was gone?

I set my jaw.

Moved back and forth with a firmer step.

I thought of Andelucia—marrying Frederick.

I stumbled and almost fell.

My shoulders slumped.

All anger gone.

The bricks twice as heavy.

Sweating freely, I finished the job.

With grim satisfaction, I noted that the back of the Packard sat considerably lower than it had before.

No longer knife and butter—the Packard would go through the bridge like flame through paper.

27

The key to the Packard was in the ignition. I shoved in the clutch and turned the key and the Packard roared to life. I joggled the gear lever and the automobile moved smoothly forward.

The hollow laugh.

The bitter snarl.

The Packard had plenty of fuel, the tires were fully aired, and the engine purred throatily. After a lifetime of living in Luck's shadow, she was smiling upon me at last.

I increased the pressure on the accelerator and the massive machine crawled out of the barn.

I caught my breath.

A fog had rolled in, cloaking the world in shrouds of filmy white. The house, halfway up the hill, was a mausoleum rising from the mist; the ravine below me was a ghostly gash in the landscape.

I was conscious of a curious ache in my soul. Partly

it was the beauty of a world wrapped in the shrouds of death, partly it was the sense of a story unfinished, a song unsung.

And yet, it was a much better thing that I was doing than, well, than not to be doing. I swung the wheel and commenced climbing the drive, engine roaring.

I remembered my hand in hers, there on the train, the musical sound of her voice as she told me that good things were going to happen, now that I was here—the wonder in her eyes as she mentioned that I led a charmed life—

I would never see her again.

A hole opened in the pit of my stomach. I could conceive of nothing worse than never to see Andelucia again.

I approached the top of the hill—

A hand touched my shoulder.

I slammed on the brakes. The Packard slewed to a stop.

"Andelucia?" I said breathlessly.

It was Bianca, of course. Bianca—who had somehow managed to slip past me and hide herself in the back seat of the Packard. She rose now, and wrapped her arms around my neck, snuggling her face close to mine—the unpleasantness of the night before somehow forgotten.

A weight lifted itself from off my shoulders.

But then I sighed the wretched sigh.

"Idiot," I said heavily. "You cannot come with me. Not where I'm going. Not this time."

Her breath tickled my ear.

I disentangled myself from her arms and stepped out of the car.

She crawled over the seat and hopped out to join me. She was more beautiful than ever, her black hair in striking contrast with the whiteness of the world around us, her creamy skin haunting and mysterious.

"Even you," I said wryly, allowing my eyes to travel freely over her contours, "with your not inconsiderable charms, are not enough to dissuade me from my course of action."

There was laughter on her lips.

Mischief in her eyes.

She moved closer to me.

"Idiot," I muttered huskily, discovering that I was not entirely immune to her charms. "You utterly adorable idiot. I'm locking you in with Grandfather."

We descended the drive to the house and I remembered a similar homecoming, a homecoming filled with wild hope.

I thinned my lips.

28

My progress was impeded at the front door.

It was Daphne.

"Good morning, Doctor," she said, looking up at me with a wistful smile.

I stared at her.

Presumably she had taken leave of her senses in the middle of the night as there could be no other rationale for her speaking to me.

"I believe congratulations are in order," she said.

I moved my mouth but nothing happened.

"I'm off to get myself engaged," she explained mournfully. "To Fishface."

Her eyes were even bluer than I remembered, and her golden curls were in delightful disarray.

She sighed heavily. "I mean Frederick."

She was wearing a blue sundress that matched the

color of her eyes. Her shoulders were plump and charming.

Possibly I looked confused.

"It's this way, Doctor," she said earnestly. "My dislike of Fishface has merely been a—a ruse to mask my broken heart."

The brave smile on her lips was at complete variance with the distress in her eyes.

"I am going to have a new sash for my dress, and butter with every meal, and oh! Doctor—do I *have* to kiss him?"

I worked my mouth again. "Andelucia," I managed. "Andelucia is going to marry Frederick. She's going to marry him and everything is ruined. Andelucia."

It seemed a point worth nailing down.

Daphne held my gaze a moment longer. "Doctor," she said earnestly, "when I get back from being engaged, do you think you could—that is, would you mind very much if—what I mean to say is this: do you think you could shower my brow with kisses?"

Her blue eyes were very blue.

I stared at her.

"Thank you, Doctor!" She pressed my hand. "It would mean a lot to me. Remember—my brow with kisses!"

And with another speaking look and the hint of a dimple she was on her way.

I turned to watch her go and observed a figure approaching through the mist. It was Frederick, moving with a marked lack of enthusiasm.

I continued on my way to Grandfather's room.

Pensive.

Profoundly thoughtful.

"You know, Bianca," I mused, patting the hand that was attached to my arm, "perhaps I've been a trifle hasty."

She smiled encouragingly at the sound of my voice.

I stared out of Grandfather's window at a world veiled in white. I could make out the barn below. I would have to remember to shut the door after I had parked the Packard. Closer at hand was an aspen. Frederick and Daphne were standing beneath the tree. They appeared to be engaged in earnest conversation.

"After all," I said, "Grandfather needs a doctor. It wouldn't be fair to him—or to Andelucia. Or to you."

Clarissa—well, accidents did happen. It was just her bad luck to be at the wrong place at the wrong time.

And, of course, I really couldn't leave Andelucia.

Not now.

Not yet.

Presently, I patted the hand that continued to grace my arm. "I like it here, Bianca—I really do. In real life, people avoid me like the plague. Well, no, that isn't exactly true. The truth is they don't even see me. In real life, well, in real life I have no life. But here—here it's different. I'm someone here. I like it here."

Bianca tilted her head, as though weighing my every word and finding each one to be of superior importance.

"You poor thing," I said. "I'm no doctor, but it's obvious something bad has happened to you. Maybe we should try to figure out what it is—after Daphne is proposed to, I mean."

Bianca continued to gaze upon me adoringly.

"How long," I wondered aloud, "do proposals usually take?"

I did not expect an answer, of course.

Nevertheless, I received one, in the form of creaking floorboards, as of someone approaching.

"Ah, Daphne," I said carelessly. "I'll bet she's forgotten all about her funny little request."

I moved towards the door.

29

It was not, after all, Daphne.

"Evangeline?"

Evangeline's gray eyes were wide and staring.

Bianca tried to hide behind me.

"Everything is ruined," Evangeline said listlessly.

She probably wanted another hug. I wondered if this was what it felt like to be a father—wiping away the tears, calming the fears, providing the occasional shoulder to cry upon. I felt strangely mature. "I once thought so myself, not too long ago," I said kindly. "But lately I've been inclined to think that everything only happens for the best. It's like an epiphany I've had. Have you seen Daphne?"

Evangeline moved blindly towards me, and the uncertainty of her step, the staggering of her forward motion, caused me to wonder if she had suffered a blow to the head. Arms hanging limply at her sides, she fell against me. "Oh, Doctor," she snuffled into my shirt. "She wasn't supposed to die." Her words were vaporish, her tone vacant. "I—oh, Doctor!"

I stroked her burning-ember hair in a fatherly fashion. She smelled faintly of thyme and rosemary. "You know, I've been thinking about that. It seems to me that Clarissa is actually better off now. She won't have to endure a marriage she doesn't want. She'll never have to worry about growing old and fat. And soldier boys are, as I'm sure you are well aware, quite scarce in these parts."

"Not Clarissa," choked Evangeline. "Daphne."

I withdrew my hand from her hair. "Daphne? Don't talk nonsense. Daphne is getting proposed to, and after she's gotten proposed to I'm going to shower her brow with—Daphne? Don't be ridiculous! Come here. I'll show you. Frederick is down there, and so is Daphne, and they're—"

"The Packard," sobbed Evangeline, and a millstone suddenly and inexplicably attached itself to my neck. "The Packard rolled down the hill and it knocked her down and now she's dead."

The world rocked to and fro.

"No," I said hoarsely.

"Yes," sobbed Evangeline.

"She wasn't supposed to die." The words scraped out of my throat, cracked and bleeding.

"I know, Doctor—oh, I know!"

A casing of lead enclosed me. "Although it is kind of habit forming, I guess. First Clarissa, now Daphne. It's anybody's guess who's going to be next."

Grandfather uttered a gurgle that I couldn't be bothered with.

Evangeline looked at me with trembling eyes. "Doctor, I'm scared—what shall I do?"

"Do?" I uttered the hollow laugh. "Why, that's easy—stay as far away from me as possible."

Evangeline snuggled closer. "Oh, Doctor—I would never hurt you."

"And I would never hurt you either," I said bitterly, "but accidents do happen."

"I know," said Evangeline in a small voice. "Oh, I forgot to tell you—Andi wants you."

"In a pig's eye."

"About Daphne."

"Oh. Yes. Of course."

"Now."

I groaned.

30

I stood like a statue as clouds tumbled across the sky and shadows on the dining room walls came to macabre life, staring at the girl whose life I had ruined. Andelucia was gazing absently out the window, the hair framing her profile exquisitely. She had been quiet and withdrawn as we conveyed Daphne to the mausoleum and laid her to temporary rest beside her sister. Sebastian was going to have his hands full upon his return.

Luck had favored the Packard. It had missed the tree beneath which Frederick and Daphne had been standing. It had missed the barn. It had even missed the ravine, coming to a rest at the bottom of the hill just below the barn. But it had not missed Daphne, and now she was dead.

Because I had killed her.

"Almost," said Andelucia softly. "Almost, it is

more than flesh and blood can bear."

There was nothing I could say.

Andelucia turned a wan smile to me. "I know why they're dead."

A thunderbolt to the soul.

"I suppose it was only a matter of time," I said dully, "before I was found out."

"Everything happens for a reason, and there's a reason for everything that happens," said Andelucia. "I killed them."

"I—you—*what?*"

Andelucia gazed at me steadily. "You see, Doctor, I have been trying to avoid doing something. I've been trying to shirk my duty—and I'm not usually a shirker. It's just that I—I kept hoping there was another way." She sighed brokenly. "But it's no use. I see that now. If I hadn't shirked, Clarissa and Daphne would be alive today. Both of them. Alive."

I uttered the sharp bark of laughter. "Don't count on it. It was I who killed them. Not you. Me. The only way they would have been alive today is if I hadn't been born."

"It's a hard lesson for me to learn, Doctor. You must think pretty poorly of me."

I stared at her. "Poorly? Of you? I—you—are you crazy? I think you're—why, I think you're—"

The smile became rueful. "Do you believe in luck,

Doctor?"

"I think you're the—*luck?*" My brain slewed sideways and I laughed the curdling laugh. "I can tell you a thing or two about luck so don't get me started on luck because if you do I'll tell you just exactly what I think about luck! Luck!"

"Exactly!" said Andelucia. "If everything was luck—if everything was the result of random chance—none of this would make any sense."

"I can talk about luck from now until Doomsday!"

"There has to be a purpose. Sometimes we might not understand what that purpose is, but there is always a reason."

I frowned. "I thought you wanted to talk about luck—"

Andelucia gave me a wistful look. "It was very sweet of you, Doctor, to give Bianca a ride in the Packard."

My jaw became unhinged and in the ensuing silence chimes sounded faintly.

Evangeline gasped and took an involuntary step towards me. Bianca, misunderstanding, shied like a startled hare. "It's Clarissa and Daphne!" bleated Evangeline. "They've come back as ghosts to haunt us!"

Andelucia sighed. "It's the wind, Evangeline."

"But don't people come back to haunt you if they die and—and it wasn't an accident?"

"Clarissa and Daphne are not coming back."

Again the chimes sounded, a ghostly sound, wavering and dying.

"The wind," said Andelucia firmly. "The wind is picking up. It's blustery outside. It's the wind, Evangeline."

I cleared my throat. "Unless it's Sebastian."

"That's even worse!" shrieked Evangeline. "If he finds out that I killed Clarissa and Daphne he'll never speak to me again! Tell him to go away!"

Andelucia regarded Evangeline thoughtfully. "We're all a little wrought up," she said at last. "Understandably so. Perhaps a picnic will take our mind off things."

"Picnic!" Evangeline's voice cracked at the upper end of the scale. "We can't have a picnic! We can't have an anything without Clarissa and Daphne! A *picnic!* We can't have a picnic! A picnic is cheerful, and this—this is the worst day in the world!"

"Nonsense!" said Andelucia briskly. "Besides, we haven't had breakfast and no one's going to want to sit around a table filled with empty chairs. I'll need your help in the kitchen, Evangeline, while the doctor tends to Grandfather."

"No!" wailed Evangeline. "Besides, I—I—besides, it's going to rain!"

"Then we'd better hurry. Come along."

Evangeline came along.

31

I stood there, watching the patterns shift on the dining room wall. The house felt strangely empty without Clarissa and Daphne.

Desolate.

"It's no use, Bianca," I said, taking Bianca by the arm and leading her up the stairs. "It's simply no use."

I sighed the weary sigh.

I was thinking of Andelucia's unfailing kindness. I was thinking of my own overwhelming failures.

It was more than flesh and blood could bear.

"Just when hope blossoms, Luck comes along and whacks it off at the knees," I said bitterly. "I can't seem to thwart it, try as I might. Luck invariably wins and there's not a thing that I can do about it."

Bianca looked at me with melting eyes.

I gripped the stair rail. "Idiot!" I said huskily. "Have you forgotten what it does to me when you look at me like that? When you look at me like that I want to throw caution to the winds and wrap you in my arms and hold you close and stroke your hair and touch your cheek and—and I want to shower your dumb brow with kisses!"

Her eyes told me that she would follow me to the ends of the earth and back.

I glared at her, but then I smiled crookedly. "Oddly enough," I said, "the way you look at me is just exactly the way I feel about your sister. Isn't that a riot? Probably there is no one in the world as beautiful as you, yet my heart is still drawn to Andelucia. Bizarre, isn't it? Well, I won't ask you to follow me to the ends of the earth, but I will ask you to play a little game with me."

Bianca looked at me expectantly.

"It's called Find the Gun. You know—gun, as in bang, bang, you're dead. You go that way and I'll go this way."

I proceeded down the hall.

Bianca tagged along.

I sighed.

"Then we'll look together."

32

I felt awkward, prowling about in Clarissa's room. Like I was violating her memory or trespassing upon the echoes of her life.

The frayed gowns.

The jewelry.

The pictures cut from magazines, elegant French fashions, pinned to the wall.

The combs, the brushes, the rouge, the—

We did not find the gun.

"Bianca?"

She poked her head out from beneath the covers.

"You're not much help, Bianca," I said sternly.

Daphne's room—

Bright sundresses, strewn about.

Romantic novels.

Scarves and a diary written in with a flowery hand. Combs and brushes.

"Blast," I muttered.

Bianca jumped out of the closet, as though to startle me.

"You are acting like a six-year-old," I said severely. "This is serious. I'm going to kill someone. I'm going to kill him dead. He should have died a long, long time ago. Why? Because as long as this person lives bad things happen—that's why, since you didn't ask."

Bianca ran over to me and touched my cheek with her fingertips, then darted quickly away, the light touching her curves.

"Imbecile!"

I banged open the doors to several closets. Sewing room, library, study. All of them failed to yield the gun.

I had no choice.

Andelucia's room looked just as I would have imagined it. Feminine without being frilly. Sensible without being severe. Clothes hung tidily, shoes lined up in a neat row, and curtains open wide to let in the day.

I opened the drawers of her dresser.

I averted my eyes at the sight of garments I had no business viewing. I felt vile and contemptible, doing what I was doing, yet I pressed on. The next-to-last drawer yielded embroidered handkerchiefs. Beneath the handkerchiefs was a packet of letters, tied up with a ribbon.

I stared at the framed photograph beneath the letters. The photograph was of a young man, strikingly handsome. His arm was around Andelucia.

I replaced the letters and slowly closed the drawer.

Hesitated.

A long moment.

I reopened the drawer.

The young man was laughing, his head thrown back, the breeze pulling at his hair. Andelucia was looking at him with austere aloofness.

I trembled.

I was lying to myself, of course. She was looking at him the way Bianca looked at me.

Something within me withered and died.

I—

"Horatio."

I jumped.

It was Andelucia, standing there beside me where she had no business standing. The floorboards had betrayed me by failing to announce her approach.

"I was—I was just—" I croaked.

Andelucia smiled wistfully. "We were to have been married. We had it all planned out. I loved him and he loved me, but it—it wasn't meant to be."

"I was looking for something. For the—for a—for something. That's why I'm here. In your bedroom, I mean."

She relieved me of the picture and studied the image

with tender eyes. "He did love me," she said. "I know he loved me."

"I told Bianca we wouldn't find it here," I said sternly, taking Bianca by the arm. "I tried to tell her. I told her we would find it somewhere else."

"The picnic is ready," said Andelucia. "If you'll just turn around I'll change into something more suitable."

She was still in her pajamas, a comfortable cream-colored flannel decorated with a pattern of small roses. She put the picture down and her fingers went to the buttons of her top.

"I—I was just—I was just leaving," I said, scuttling for the door.

33

In the gray-green distance mountain tops, white and brittle, touched the lowering skies. There was something breathtaking in their distant majesty—something removed from the cares of the world. It was as though one could climb across the intervening peaks, one step at a time, and touch the brow of heaven.

"It's the reason my grandparents built the house here," said Andelucia comfortably. "The view is only visible from this side of the house. There's nothing quite like it."

"Nothing in the world," I murmured, but I was looking at Andelucia and I was thinking how extraordinary it was that she had made no reference to my being in her room and getting into her things and being where I had no business being.

Andelucia moved closer to me. "I used to think I could climb across those peaks to the brow of heaven, one step at a time. And maybe I will someday, to say hello to—to my sisters."

"That's just what I was—" A slender ribbon of hope wove its spell around me once more and I stared at her intently. "Have you ever felt a—a connection with someone? A kindred spirit? With a—well, like with a man, I mean—with someone you'd only known a short time?"

Andelucia gave me a quizzical look. "Did Daphne tell you about Gregory?"

"What I mean is, did you ever feel a—who's Gregory?"

Andelucia's gaze slipped once more to the horizon, and a mournful smile took possession of her face. "I thought in Gregory I had found True Love. He was my world, and I was his."

"Gregory?"

"My first love. There have only been three, and the third one is hardest of all." There was a catch in her voice.

"I see," I said numbly. "Your True—I'm sorry I mentioned it."

There was a moment of silence, broken as Andelucia made an observation. "You know, I sometimes think she's the lucky one."

She was looking at Bianca.

"She's an idiot!" I said sharply.

Andelucia gave me her arm. "No inhibitions, completely oblivious to grief and sorrow—no affairs of the heart to crush and destroy—and feet as tough as nails. Oh, once a month she gets a little mopey, once a month she gets a little grumpy, but otherwise—no worries."

"She's an imbecile!"

Andelucia smiled at me, and I shuddered with the warmth of it. "She's showing off for you, you know. She loves you, Doctor. I haven't seen her this happy in ages."

Bianca was romping beneath a sprawling Ponderosa pine, flinging her arms in the air, prancing like a colt in springtime, her body in marvelous motion, wonderfully uninhibited, wonderfully—

I looked away abruptly. "What she needs," I said harshly, "is to put some clothes on!"

"It's so good to have you here with us, Doctor," said Andelucia softly.

I laughed the bitter laugh. "If I had known then what I know now I never would have come."

"I see," said Andelucia, drawing away from me. "Well, perhaps we should eat."

Evangeline had spread a checkered cloth and laid out the contents of a large wicker basket. We seated ourselves, making the distant horizon our view, and I accepted a tasteless hard-boiled egg and a thin slice of equally tasteless buttered toast.

It wasn't the food—it was me. Food was as ashes in

my mouth.

"Much better, Evangeline," complimented Andelucia, pouring herself another cup of tea from the chilled crock.

Evangeline lifted tragic eyes to her sister and said nothing.

We ate in silence, while high above us birds chirped a discouragingly cheerful roundelay. Despite Andelucia's intentions, the weight of sorrow hung heavily upon us.

Except for Bianca, of course. She popped over to me from time to time in order to take a bite from my toast or nibble on my egg before scampering off to frolic.

"You know," mused Andelucia, helping herself to a second piece of toast, "perhaps it was all for the best."

Evangeline looked startled and I caught my breath.

"No," said Andelucia quickly. "I was thinking of Horatio."

Evangeline's expression resumed its mask of grief.

"When Horatio broke my heart I had no way of knowing that Mom and Dad would soon be taken from us. I couldn't have foreseen that Grandfather would take sick. And then Bianca, and now Clarissa and Daphne. You see, Doctor, it wouldn't have worked at all."

I forced down another bite of egg.

"I guess it just goes to show," continued Andelucia thoughtfully, "that everything happens for the best. And somehow, someway, perhaps we'll look back and recognize just how right this is."

Her voice became uneven.

I shifted my shoulders uncomfortably, because Bianca seemed to be climbing on them.

Andelucia fetched me a haunting smile, then addressed Bianca. "Not now, honey. Perhaps when the doctor is finished he can give you a piggyback ride."

I stared at her. "Are you kidding? A—are you out of your mind? With Bianca? Are you completely—? Not a chance!"

Andelucia touched me with her glance. "It would mean so much to her, Doctor."

"No! Absolutely not!"

"While Evangeline and I tidy up, of course," said Andelucia briskly.

Evangeline stared bleakly at nothing.

I swallowed my last bite.

Bianca encircled my neck with her arms.

I rose and she flung her legs around my waist. I trembled with her weight and hooked my arms beneath her knees. It was contact of such delicacy that I shuddered. Nevertheless, I bent forward, shifting her weight, and gave an experimental trot.

Bianca uttered an unexpected squeal of joy.

I smiled in spite of myself, then trotted in earnest, head down, running blindly up and down the lawn.

I slowed quickly, puffing like a steam engine.

Appearances can be deceiving. Although Bianca looked like some feathery sprite or a shaft of creamy moonlight, the reality was that she weighed a ton.

Sweat beaded on my brow, and Bianca's legs became slippery in my arms. I recognized the wisdom in bringing our romp to an end.

Andelucia was smiling. "Bianca is having the time of her life."

Her praise lent strength to my limbs and I exerted myself once more, galloping off round the pine at a dizzying pace.

Despite her weight and the heart-constricting contact of her bare skin—despite everything—I was conscious of a glow, a sense of well-being. It was incongruous, of course, but I had found a place I would like to call home. If I could stop myself from executing everyone in sight I could almost see myself forging a future here. A few chickens. A pig. Maybe a cow. With a little work, the place could pay for itself. Maybe the past could fade and eventually be forgotten. Maybe. Maybe I could make a life here with Andelucia and Bianca and Evangeline and Grandfather and—

I heard a peculiar noise—like someone thumping for ripeness a green melon. A tremor went through Bianca and her hands released their hold around my neck; she became a dead weight on my back, throwing me off balance. I pranced frantically to and fro, making a desperate bid for equilibrium, but I was being pulled backwards—backwards—

34

I opened my eyes. Above me, fanning the sky, were the branches of the pine. Birds rent the air with their ceaseless songs. Beyond the perimeter of branches clouds chased each other with reckless abandon across a deep blue sky. I felt peculiarly comfortable, and a feeling of deep peace stole over me.

"Doctor," said Andelucia urgently, standing above me with a strained expression.

She appeared careworn. Bowed with the weight of responsibility. It bothered me that she should be shouldering the weight of so great a burden alone. I felt I should help her. I should provide support.

Comfort.

I should encourage her.

"Everything will turn out all right," I said soothingly. "You'll see. There's a future here. Chickens. A pig. Maybe a cow. Everything always happens for the best. Sometimes we just have to—"

"Bianca!"

"Bianca." A frown creased my brow. "That's funny. I don't see her. I wonder where she could have gone off to. And here's another funny thing—why am I lying on the ground?"

"Get off her!"

Andelucia grabbed my hand and hauled me to my feet.

I blushed. "Oh," I said. "I see. That's why I was so—why is she resting?"

"She's dead!" screamed Evangeline. "Bianca's dead! She's dead—dead—*dead!*"

There was a purplish lump on Bianca's brow, oozing blood.

"What happened?" I asked, puzzled, as Andelucia bent over Bianca. "Did a bridge fall on her? Did she get hit by a car?"

And then I perceived above us a low branch and I knew what had happened. Iron gavels hammered my lungs.

"You killed her!" snarled Evangeline. Strangely glittering eyes bored into mine. "It's been you all along, hasn't it? Clarissa. Daphne. It's been you! *You* killed them!" Her freckles stood out like oysters. "And now Bianca's stone-cold dead! Who's next, Doctor? Who are you going to knock off next? You're running low on options, Doctor!"

The tone was mocking, vicious.

I took an involuntary step backwards in the face of such unexpected hostility.

"Evangeline!" snapped Andelucia.

"I—I'm a pariah," I said mournfully.

"You're in big trouble is what you are, buster," seethed Evangeline, and her eyes were shards of slate. "You've ruined everything! You're going to pay, you murderer you!"

"That's enough, Evangeline!" Andelucia's voice splintered the air. "Bianca is not dead!"

"She's not?" I started to breathe again.

"Then she will be soon," spat Evangeline, "if the doctor here has his way!"

"To your room, Evangeline." Andelucia's voice was steel. "*Now!*"

Evangeline gave me a venomous look. "Big trouble," she hissed before dashing to the house.

"I believe it's just a mild concussion, Doctor, but we should get her inside. Do you think you could carry her to your bed? I'd like you to keep an eye on her, if it wouldn't be too much trouble."

"Well, she's alive, at any rate," I said briskly. "That's something. It means I didn't kill her because she's alive."

"Evangeline didn't mean anything by what she

said," said Andelucia gently. "It's just that we've been under a lot of stress lately. Poor Evangeline hasn't really been herself since it became obvious that one of us was going to have to marry Frederick. Mother and Father were taken from us at a bad time and I don't think she's prepared to lose a sister. And, of course, now she's lost two. She's just a little wrought up, Doctor."

I lifted Bianca into my arms and cradled her close.

"This shouldn't be me," I murmured softly. "This should be your husband, carrying you to your nuptial bed."

"Excuse me, Doctor?"

"She's not going to die," I said firmly. "She can't die. It wouldn't be fair."

"Of course she's not going to die, Doctor," said Andelucia kindly. "It's just a bump on the head. Like last time. Sebastian carrying her back from the bridge, the blood running down her face, her temple swelling. It was my fault, really. I shouldn't have let her beg me into going to town for groceries. Always before I had gone. It was my responsibility. I let her go, taking the motorbike—with the sidecar for the groceries, of course. Sebastian found her. The motorbike and sidecar had gone over the side of the bridge and into the ravine. Why she lost control of the motorbike is something we'll probably never know—or, for that matter, why she now hates men and refuses to wear clothes."

Bianca's tears at the bridge finally made some sense. I held her a little closer. "If she doesn't die then that means I didn't murder her, doesn't it?"

Andelucia touched my arm. "We've all been through a lot and you've borne it stoically. You've seen us at our worst and you haven't flinched. I can't thank you enough for being here. You've been so good to us—ooh, you almost dropped her there."

"I'm fine," I grunted.

We entered the house.

35

I laid Bianca gently on my bed. Her breathing was shallow, but she was breathing. So was I, but just barely. My arms had long since gone to water, and the magic of her skin against my fingers had turned to agony. I rolled my shoulders, trying to work the kinks out of my neck and restore feeling to my arms. My lower back ached.

I did not run to fetch cold compresses.

Because Andelucia was wrong.

Bianca was going to die.

It was as inevitable as the setting of the sun.

It wasn't Fate.

It wasn't Destiny.

It was just my bad luck.

But I wouldn't be around for her passing.

I tendered Bianca a long, last, lingering look, then went resolutely back down the stairs.

I found the gun with ridiculous ease. It was under some pillowcases in the bottom drawer of Andelucia's dresser.

Cold and heavy and utterly repulsive.

I put the gun to my head.

I paused.

Not here.

Not in Andelucia's room.

I lowered the gun and trotted up the stairs and back into my room.

Bianca continued to breathe shallowly.

I sighed, damped a cloth, and sponged the abrasion on her head. She did not stir.

I watched her for some time before going into Grandfather's room and shutting the door behind me forever.

Again I put the weapon to my head, staring out the window as low clouds threw the world into shadow. Leaves flickered white in the wind and the lawn moved like a serpent.

No one interrupted me. The floorboards were silent. Evangeline was elsewhere. Bianca was as good as dead. Grandfather hadn't moved since the last time I had seen him.

I had but to the pull the trigger and my bad luck would be at a permanent end. More importantly, Andelucia would not have to worry about losing any more of her family.

And yet, I hesitated. There was still the sense of a song unsung, a story—

I needed closure.

I scratched my ear with the barrel of my weapon.

"This is what I should have done in the first place," I told Grandfather conversationally. "Actually, it's what Bianca should have done when she had the chance. Sometimes it's better that one should die instead of someone's whole family being massacred."

Grandfather did not respond.

"And this time," I said harshly, "I will not be stopped. I won't be thwarted, nor will I be distracted. Quick and simple, bang!—I wish I had thought of this earlier."

Grandfather continued to evince a complete lack of interest.

I almost thought of Andelucia. She was preparing to meet Frederick so he could propose to her and I knew that it would be the biggest mistake of her tragic life but there wasn't a thing I could do about it, so I closed the door on the thought before it could even be properly formed. I locked myself away in a cocoon of numbness.

Of darkness.

I placed the gun against my temple.

I was ready.

"To Luck," I muttered.

I pulled the—
I frowned and moved closer to the window.
Someone was coming down the drive.
It was Frederick, draped in a greatcoat.
It wasn't Frederick.
It was Sebastian.

36

Ever have a moment in which the world hits a pothole and plows into a tree? I was shaking so badly I could hardly see straight. Cold fury possessed me. The source of all my problems, the cause of every single bad thing that had ever happened to me in my whole entire life was strolling nonchalantly down the drive with nary a care in the world.

I would kill him.

I would rip him limb from limb and I would wipe that smug, confident, self-assured smirk right off his smug, confident face and I would keep on killing him until he was stone-cold dead, and then I would kill him some more. I could almost feel my hands around his throat, squeezing the life out of him, which is how I nearly put a hole in the wainscoting. I eased up on the trigger and barged out of Grandfather's room.

I paused.

I popped back into my room to check once more on Bianca. I had a feeling I wouldn't be back and she deserved this much—

She looked so peaceful lying there, so lovely in repose, that I found myself leaving another kiss upon her ivory brow. "I'm going to make things right," I informed her grimly, and then I was out of the room and charging down the stairs, two at a time.

"Doctor," said Andelucia, waylaying me in the parlor. She had on a gray raincoat and was occupied with tucking her brown hair into a gray rain cap. There was a peculiar note in her voice.

"Busy," I said brusquely.

She appeared not to have heard. She turned to me, and tilted her head to one side. "You wouldn't happen to be independently wealthy, would you?" The look in her eyes was incomprehensible.

"What? Of course not! In fact, I'm—look, I'm really quite busy at the moment and you're interrupting me, so if you'll just excuse me—"

I did not deem it necessary to tell her that her continued existence rendered my financial future bleak indeed.

Her quizzical smile faded. "Oh! Quite. Sorry to have troubled you."

I moved towards the door.

"Doctor?" The word was a whisper of sound.

"What!"

"Nothing."

A final time I headed for the door.

At the door a clumsy bloke with red hair and a great-coat failed to see me. I was knocked to the floor.

Seriously!

I lay there.

Winded.

Stunned.

But, of course, it was more than that. I could not, for the life of me, chart a course without something coming along and derailing all of my carefully laid plans. I could not set my hand to the plow without an upheaval of cataclysmic proportions shoving me way off course.

Andelucia extended her hand and I fumbled my hand into it. Her skin was smooth and soft and the look she gave me I did not understand at all.

She helped me to my feet.

I glared at her.

I turned to Sebastian.

I paused.

He was bigger than I remembered. More formidable. Humongous-er. His expression disturbed me. A gun would have come in handy just now, but I no longer seemed to have one. I wondered if I had dropped it when I was knocked to the floor, but I didn't think so. I tried to remember when I had had it last.

"Sebastian—you big oaf," said Andelucia kindly.

Sebastian removed his gaze from me. "Andelucia," he said slowly. "You're looking well."

His words were weighted with significance.

"Thank you, I am quite well."

Sebastian's eyes probed the points of the room. "I am given to understand that Bianca has met with an unfortunate accident. Blow to the head. Unconscious. Confined, if I understand correctly, to her room. Is it safe?"

"Perfectly." A wry smile touched the corners of Andelucia's mouth. "I apprehend that Evangeline did not, after all, go straight to her room."

"I also understand that congratulations are shortly to be in order."

Andelucia shrugged. "I have no choice, Sebastian. We are at an *impasse*. You know I will not sell."

"And I will not be made responsible for Bianca! Or for Grandfather either, for that matter." Sebastian drew a deep breath. "But of course, you know that."

"Perfectly, brother," said Andelucia.

"Then Bianca isn't the only idiot around here," said Sebastian harshly.

"As you will."

There was an uncomfortable pause.

"Under the bridge?" inquired Sebastian.

"No. Overlooking the glen."

"Speaking of the bridge, the blasted driver refused to drive across it. Hasn't the county repaired that blasted thing yet?"

"Not yet, no."

"It's going to rain, you know."

"Yes, I do believe it's going to rain some."

"It's your funeral." Sebastian gave his broad shoulders a negligent shrug.

"I would like, upon my return, to discuss one or two things with you."

Sebastian smiled tightly. "Like why the Packard is at the bottom of the hill instead of parked in the barn?"

"And how one of your guns showed up unexpectedly," said Andelucia. "I'll be back within the hour."

"Very well," said Sebastian. "I'll look in on Grandfather."

"Do that," said Andelucia. "I think you'll find the good doctor here has been quite competent in his care of him. And I believe, also thanks to the good doctor, that you will find Bianca a changed girl."

She stepped out of the house and moved towards the barn, and I was struck by something in her carriage. I couldn't place it at first, but then I had it. It seemed indicative of a young girl in a tumbril, on her way to the guillotine.

37

Sebastian did not immediately go and check on Grandfather. Instead, he enclosed my arm in a vice-like grip and hauled me through the house and out the back door.

"Good doctor, indeed," he hissed at me. "Angel tells me you've been killing everyone in sight! Clarissa—dead! Daphne—dead! Bianca—almost dead! And yet, I could not help but notice that Andelucia is alive and well. Extremely well, I might add." He glowered at me. "Naturally, I'm going to have to bust you up some for killing Clarissa and Daphne."

He released my arm and commenced doffing his greatcoat and rolling up his sleeves.

Thunder grumbled in the distance, and the air was oppressive. Sebastian's shoulders were broader than I remembered. Muscles stood out on his arms. I perceived that my immediate future was going to be somewhat unpleasant.

"Accidents," I said thoughtfully. "Accidents, every one. Clarissa and Daphne—they weren't supposed to die. Bianca. Not what I had intended at all. You'd be surprised how accident prone everyone is around here—now that I'm here, of course."

Sebastian snorted. "I told you Andelucia can't be killed. Goodness knows I've tried often enough. Half the doctors before you were fellows just like yourself. Well, no, not just like yourself—no one else was so unlucky as to lose with a royal flush. But, like you, they failed to kill Andelucia. Unlike you, they at least had the decency to leave everyone else alone."

I recalled Andelucia standing before the mirror in the hallway as she tucked her hair into her rain cap. I recalled the heightened color in her face, the extraordinary brightness of her hazel eyes. She was every bit as beautiful, I suddenly realized, as her sisters. A smile quirked the corner of my mouth. "It's probably the only good thing I've ever done," I murmured. "Saving her life, I mean. I can feel good about that."

"You saved someone's life? You?" A frown corrugated Sebastian's brow. "Angel's, I presume. Well, she can usually take care of herself, but if you saved her life then I'm beholden to you. I'll try not to break every bone in your face. See, Angel's the only one of the lot with a grain of sense. She's a brick."

I perceived he was referring to Evangeline.

I smiled the distant smile. "She would have choked to death, there on the train, had it not been for me."

Sebastian blinked. "Andelucia? You saved *Andelucia?* No, no, I can't say that I'm surprised—but Andelucia!"

"Andelucia," I said. "You see, I love her. I think I loved her from the first moment that I looked into her eyes. Looking into her eyes was—well, it was like finding the other half of my soul."

Sebastian stared at me. Presently, his lip twitched. Then he threw back his head and roared with laughter. Wiping tears from his eyes, he said, "Well, don't that beat all! You must be the unluckiest bloke in the world!"

"Yes, I sometimes think I must be."

"Ironic—that's what I call it! Commissioned to kill a girl—and falling head over heels for her! Ironic—that's what it is!"

I stared at him. "You're mad, of course. Andelucia is a fine, noble, wonderful—she cares for her grandfather, takes care of her sisters—what's left of them—she's doing the right thing by the memory of her grandmother and, well, she's all that is good and right in this world. Something must be terribly wrong with you for you to want to—to—"

Sebastian chuckled hugely. "You don't get it, do you? I'm not going to kill her—nobody's going to kill her. And do you know why? For the plain and simple reason that she cannot be killed." He shifted me the sideways glance. "You never even tried, did you? To kill her, I mean."

"Don't be an idiot," I said. "You know, I think she was trying to tell me something, there in the passage, before she went off to get herself engaged."

"Didn't even try," murmured Sebastian.

"There's something else I can't get out of my mind. She was going to change clothes with me in the bedroom with her. She told me to turn around, but she didn't tell me to leave the room. I'd like to think that was significant, that maybe she—but, of course, it's probably just because she's used to doctors. If I think it means something it will turn out to mean nothing."

Sebastian grinned. "So you never tried to shove her out a window? Didn't try to poison her tea, loosen the carpet runner at the top of the stairs, suffocate her with a pillow? Yet you managed somehow to kill Clarissa and Daphne. Your luck must be truly abominable."

I nodded. "You have no idea. When it comes to luck, I wrote the book. I can't blink without luck yanking the rug out from beneath me."

"Me, on the other hand—" said Sebastian expansively. "I'm the luckiest man in the world. What I want comes to me. My desires are invariably fulfilled. My hopes are always realized. Nothing is denied me. Luck lavishes me with her affection." Sebastian donned his greatcoat and snagged my arm. "Follow me—I want to show you something."

I followed, having been given no choice in the matter whatsoever.

38

Thunder rolled back and forth across the sky, low and threatening, and the breeze sharpened perceptibly. Shadows deepened, and there was the sense of something portentous in the air, something dark and foreboding.

Sebastian dragged me briskly towards the ravine, where it would probably be easier to dispose of my body after he had busted me up some. I saw now the wisdom of having gone in for the river when I had had the chance.

Instead of following the ravine, Sebastian moved beyond it, striking a course across thickly forested land.

"Shortcut," he said, breathing hard and thrashing through virgin timber that would have been rough going for a horse and rider, if not utterly impossible. I hung on for dear life.

An interminable time later, Sebastian slowed. "Keep your head down," he said. "We're here. At the overlook."

We were concealed in a mass of thick underbrush. Not more than a dozen yards in front of us the world appeared to end abruptly, and I had the impression of vast distances and great depths, a glimpse of the richly forested valley below, and beyond the valley, in the gray distance, the eternal mountains rising to meet the sky.

Between us and the edge of the world were a couple of horses, their backs to us and the wind, taking shelter beneath the sprawling limbs of a massive cottonwood. Frederick was mounted on a horse I had not seen before, a nervous palomino that seemed less than enthusiastic about the wind and rain and thunder than Daisy, who seemed impervious to the elements, placidly nibbling at the clover growing among the thick moss at her feet. Frederick was leaning towards Andelucia and seemed to be in earnest conversation with her, although it was impossible to hear what he was saying.

Somehow, simply being in Andelucia's presence brought peace to my soul. Maybe I would ask her what it was she wanted to tell me, there in the hall. Maybe I would ask her about the peculiar circumstance there in her bedroom. And maybe I would also warn her not to marry Frederick. But then I remembered that Sebastian was breathing down my neck and decided it might be better if I said nothing at all.

Sebastian reached into his capricious greatcoat.

From a shoulder holster he pulled forth a wicked-looking gun.

Anvils attached themselves to my lungs. "No!" I wheezed. "You can't! I—I won't let you!"

I was trembling, but I was also determined.

He grinned.

"I wouldn't dream of shooting her." He handed me the gun. "You're going to."

I stared at him.

"No," I protested frantically, trying desperately to hand it back. "Really. No. I can't. *No!*"

Like trying to say no to an avalanche.

"Point it at her."

"No," I begged him. "I mean it this time!"

The grin disappeared.

"Now."

I perceived again the strength of his personality.

I pointed the weapon at Andelucia.

Sebastian leaned close. "Here's the deal, Doctor," he murmured in my ear, placing unnecessary emphasis on the title. "Fire at her—and your debt is wiped clean."

39

Lightning flickered. Thunder grumbled, closer now. I nearly grinned out loud.

I could point that gun at Andelucia all day long, but no power in heaven or earth could cause me to pull the trigger. I looked at the gray raincoat and the gray rain cap and drew strength.

"Good," said Sebastian, breathing heavily in my ear. "Now, gently, gently, pull the trigger—"

Thunder rent the heavens. Sharp gusts of cool air tempered moments of restless calm.

"Not that gently, you idiot!" He scowled at me. "You don't get it, do you? You cannot comprehend how infernally lucky Andelucia is. The gun will jam. Daisy will spook—well, no, Daisy served in the Great War and nothing spooks her. But the world will twist on its axis or you'll be struck by lightning, but you will not kill her. *She cannot be killed!*"

I glanced at him. "What about you?" I asked. "Can you be killed? What's to stop me from putting a hole in your head?"

His visage darkened and I felt the menace in his brooding presence. "I'd kill you, for starters. And then I'd break all your arms and tie you into a pretzel and kill you some more."

I considered the merit in his proposal and determined that he could undoubtedly do what he promised. What was stopping me was myself. I couldn't kill him in cold blood. I saw now that I couldn't even kill myself, back in Grandfather's room. Even if I hadn't seen Sebastian coming up the drive I wouldn't have been able to pull that trigger—I would have found another excuse, another reason.

I was a coward.

It was an epiphany of sorts, but not a good one.

"Now pull the bloody—what are you grinning about?"

I wasn't grinning. I was smiling. Sebastian was a fool if he thought I was capable of shooting the one girl I loved more than life itself. I was going to tell him that Andelucia and I had a future together and he had better get used to the idea. I was going to tell him—well, I was going to tell him any number of things, and when I got through telling him he would know just how impossible it was for me to—

A blinding flash of searing blue-white light.

The detonation of a thousand suns going nova.

Electricity surging through limb and leaf and every blade of grass.

Frederick's horse rearing, whinnying desperately, throwing Frederick to the ground.

Daisy continuing to graze placidly.

And someone—or something—yanking my hand backwards.

40

The sky opened and the rain commenced coming down, slashing the world in soaking, wind-swept gusts. Lightning seared the sky, illuminating the heavens from east to west; thunder echoed and reechoed. The smell of damp earth and sodden foliage mingled with ozone.

"There. What did I tell you?" Sebastian had to raise his voice in order to be heard. Bitterness could be discerned in his tone. "I told you she can't be killed. It's uncanny—spooky! She talks about plans and designs but it's really just her blasted luck!"

"I'm not going to pull the trigger," I babbled, somewhat dazed. "I'm going to stand here all day if necessary, and all night, too, but you won't catch me pulling any ol' trigger. What just went bang?"

Sebastian chuckled. "You know, it first began to dawn on me that she couldn't be killed out there on the bridge. I had removed one of the planks, and when her motorcycle was no more than ten feet away I reared up, hideous and gibbering. Frightened the tar out of her, of course. She swerved and the motorcycle crashed right through the railing and went over the side. She tried to jump free of the bike but her dress got caught. She was absolutely frantic, but she couldn't extricate herself from that dress. And then, wouldn't you know it, the dress saved her, snagging the broken rail and ripping away from the bike as the bike fell into the ravine. She managed to bang her head up pretty good, though.

"And then, of course, it wasn't Andelucia at all. It was Bianca. What are the odds! Always before it had been Andelucia. *Always!* But not this time. Incredible, isn't it? Believe me when I say it—Andelucia cannot be killed!"

I pointed.

Andelucia was slipping forward on Daisy's neck. And then, even as we watched, she pitched forward to fall face first onto the wet, mossy ground. One side of her gray rain cap bled crimson.

Rain hammered the earth.

Sebastian stood as though hewn from stone. "Unbelievable," he muttered. "It's—no, it's simply not possible. You say you loved her?"

A raw chill crawled through my bones, as though Judgment Day had arrived and I—I without a thing to wear. "You said she couldn't be killed," I said in a voice as thin as yesterday's gruel. "You said it was impossible. You said it couldn't be done."

Sebastian thoughtfully pried my frozen fingers loose from his gun and returned it to his shoulder holster. "I blame this on you, of course. This is your fault. Never have I seen luck as terrible as yours. I should have known how it was when you lost with that royal flush. But this—this breaks all the rules. Of course I'm going to have to bust you up some for killing Andelucia. She wasn't supposed to die, you nincompoop. I'm going to have to bust you up some but good."

I swayed, and the wind and rain became a roaring in my ears. I moved my arms, reaching for something, anything, to hang on to. There was nothing—nothing but the wind and the rain and the rising tide.

A wail of indescribable grief.

Not from me.

Oddly enough.

I wondered who it could be.

41

The wail came from Frederick, who had gotten to his feet.

He beat upon his chest.

He tore at his hair.

He shrieked at the heavens.

"I killed her!" he screamed into the wind and the rain and the darkness of the day.

Sebastian arose from the concealment of the shadows and strode purposefully into the clearing. I tottered after him, not so much by choice or design, but simply because I had lost all volition and following in his wake was the path of least resistance.

"Nonsense, my good man!" said Sebastian heartily. "You had nothing to do with her death, I assure you!"

Frederick grabbed Sebastian by the lapels of his greatcoat. "I killed them all!" he frothed. "Me! It was me! I cut them down in the bloom of life and the vigor of youth! Oh, I am undone! I'm a cursed man! A dead man walking am I!"

"Here now!" Sebastian said in bracing tones. "You're blameless. The perpetrator of this heinous crime is—" His brows came slowly together. "How did you kill them?"

Frederick's eyes were stark and wild, blazing with an inner fire, his hands white-knuckled and his insignificant chest heaving. "Clarissa! Take Clarissa!" The words were an unstoppable spewing. "'Will you marry me?' That's what I asked her. I didn't want to. But I had to. She didn't want me to ask her. But she had no choice. 'Will you marry me?' I would give worlds to unsay those words! 'Will you marry me?' I asked her, and then the whole world came crashing down on her, crushing her innocence, snuffing her hopes and dreams, shattering her—!"

Sebastian grinned expansively. "Hardly your fault, old chap. You don't kill someone just by proposing to them. The doctor, now—"

"Daphne!" A vein throbbed on Frederick's brow. "Take Daphne, for instance! Just take Daphne, for a particular instance! She was young! Full of fun and frolic! I didn't want to ask her! We both knew she didn't want to be asked! I asked her anyway! I had to! I'm a desperate man, you understand! Desperate! And now—now I would give worlds! 'Will you marry me?' and before she could open those trembling lips of hers she was gone, gone, gone—taken from this realm and transported to another! Too young! Too young!"

Sebastian chuckled. "Honestly, Freddy, what were you thinking? She was a little young to be thinking of marriage! But never mind that now. Fortunately, the doctor here should be able to shed some light on these unfortunate occurrences—"

Frederick's words became guttural and unnatural. "And now—just now," he said thickly. "I warned her! 'Every time,' I told her, 'someone dies! Horribly! Unexpectedly! Inevitably!' I *told* her! She—she begged me to say them. 'Third time's a charm,' she said. 'You'll die!' I yelled. 'Won't either,' she said. 'Will!' I said. 'Won't,' she said. And then she said, 'I can't die—you'll see! The others died because—well, because things were different with them. But I won't die because—well, because things are different for me and I can't die.' 'You can!' I told her. 'Can't,' she said. 'Can!' I roared. 'I love you,' she said. 'What?' I said. 'Propose to me, you goof,' she said. 'Marry me,' I said, and then she—she's gone! She's struck by lightning and she's dead and she's gone and I think I will go out of my mind with madness!"

And he wailed anew in the depths of his grief and in the pit of his black sorrow.

"Yes," said Sebastian, thoughtfully prying Frederick's fingers loose from his lapel. He nudged the body with his foot, and I experienced an unreasonable desire to obliterate him from the face of the earth. "I see what you mean. Unpredictable thing, lightning. Deadly, rather. Pity. Well, accidents do happen." He employed his foot with greater vigor and forced the body over.

Rain grayed the distance and blurred the foreground. Again the feeling of being swept along by an evil tide—

Sebastian seemed to sway. "Angel," he said huskily, and his voice was a vaporish thing.

42

Evangeline.

Dead.

I had, inexplicably and incredibly, killed Evangeline.

She who had come to me for comfort had died at my hand. She who had pummeled my chest, she who had rested her mint-and-thyme-scented hair beneath my chin—she who had sought me out to comfort her troubled soul—

I had killed her.

In cold blood.

"Angel!" Sebastian wailed, sinking to the ground like a wounded man, cradling the gray-capped head to his breast. "O, my Angel!" His tears mingled with the rain and joined a river of crimson. "You weren't meant to die! Never you! My precious sister, my darling Angel—no!"

My thoughts turned to Andelucia. I wondered at how my arrival had precipitated nothing but heartache and grief.

I could not face her again.

Not now.

Not ever.

I could not face those hazel eyes ever again.

"You—!" choked Sebastian, his face contorted by a grief beyond my comprehension. "You *fiend!*"

"Maybe," I suggested woodenly, "she's just resting."

"You just put a bloody hole through her head!" yelled Sebastian.

"Probably not, then."

"Go!" roared Sebastian. "Go! And leave me to my—just go!"

I hesitated.

"Freddy will take you!" Sebastian rocked back and forth, the sodden ground and the driving rain the canvas upon which he was etched. "Freddy knows the way. Now *go!*"

He bowed his head over the lifeless figure and his shoulders shook convulsively.

We went.

43

I entered the house and dripped quietly on the floor. Frederick had been detained momentarily in the barn with the palomino. He had been profoundly thoughtful on the way back, and I—I, too, had been busy with my thoughts.

The house was quiet, too quiet, as though life had been torn from the structure. The windows let in little light; darkened walls pressed in on me.

I escaped into the dining room, unsure as to what to do or where to go, or even why I was there.

"Why, hello, Doctor."

It was Andelucia. I remembered now that I wasn't going to return, but somehow I had and it was too late to do anything about it now. She approached and the room brightened with her presence. Her face was flushed, her color high.

My insides lurched and a nameless pain wrapped

itself around me.

"I found that, after all, I just couldn't do it," Andelucia said breathlessly. She touched my arm impulsively. "I know everything happens for a reason and there's a reason for everything that happens—but sometimes you just have to do what you *know* is right and hope for the best. I found that I couldn't—well, I sent Evangeline to tender my apologies. Actually, she insisted on going."

Her eyes were stars in heaven.

"Oh, hello, Frederick. I didn't see you come in. Did Evangeline speak to you? I find that I cannot, after all, but of course Evangeline told you all about it." She flashed me a radiant smile. "You see, Doctor, I—is everything all right?"

The sullen rain played a mournful dirge on the window pane and the sound of it filled the silence.

Presently I cleared my throat.

"Evangeline," I said. "Well, she's dead, of course."

The words were more flippant than I had intended, my delivery not quite what I would have desired.

Shock and surprise battled for supremacy on Andelucia's countenance. She sank into a chair, the color leaving her face, the light fading from her eyes.

"You just can't tell about some people," I offered, "until it's too late and, of course, by then they have wreaked indescribable havoc."

"Dead." Her voice was steady enough, but her eyes trembled. "Evangeline, did you say? Yes, yes, of course. Evangeline. Dead." Now the words came with some difficulty. "No, it cannot be. It is too much. Not—no, it is not so."

"Ironically," I said, "we thought it was you. The gray raincoat. The gray rain hat. It had to be you. It *was* you. But, no, it wasn't you."

"It should have been me," said Andelucia bleakly. "I see that now. And yet, I knew. I knew I could not—I *knew!* Once more, the cup of happiness at my lips. Once more, whacked off at the knees. O, Doctor!" Her expression reached out to me.

I drew close. "It was the lightning," I murmured. "Otherwise—and you must believe me—otherwise, I never would have pulled the—"

She was trembling, as though in shock, her eyes begging me to relieve her of her grief.

I placed my hand upon her shoulder.

The contact, insignificant though it was, gave wings to my soul.

She covered my hand with hers, a cold and shaking hand, a hand that gripped mine with peculiar intensity. "Doctor," she said, lifting her head, her eyes looking into my soul, "I'm so glad it wasn't you. You're alive. I don't think I could have borne it had anything happened to—Doctor?"

"I'm fine," I said huskily. "Just a momentary—I'm fine." I may have increased the pressure on her shoulder in an effort to remain upright. She bore it unflinchingly.

"And I, too, am alive," she said thoughtfully. "I am spared. To what end, I cannot say—nevertheless, I live."

Frederick stepped forward a pace. "As to that, perhaps I can help you out," he said. "Sebastian says—well, he says many things, but he says I'm not to blame for Evangeline's death, and he also says that perhaps I'm not to blame for Daphne or Clarissa's deaths either. So, if that's the case, and all else being equal—will you marry me?"

44

Empires rose and fell between the proposal and Andelucia's answer.

Andelucia lowered her eyes. "Of course," she murmured, and some of the life went out of her. "It's come to this. I suppose it was inevitable. Plan and design usually are. Everything points to one inevitable conclusion. Despite all that I can do, despite all that I have done."

Frederick looked confused. "Is that a yes or a no?"

Andelucia gave him a wan smile. "I don't seem to have much choice in the—is that someone at the door?"

It was Sebastian.

He entered the room, shaking off the wind and the rain from his greatcoat. There was a grimness about him that had not been in evidence before. The jaunty demeanor, the careless grin, the lightness in his step—these things were gone. In their place was a brooding darkness, a heaviness of spirit. "Your bag, Doctor," he said. "We are leaving."

The earth shifted in its course, and I leaned heavily on Andelucia. Her shoulder tightened, but when she spoke her voice was calm. "Sebastian, you just got here. You can't leave just yet. We haven't discussed—various matters. Besides, the girls need to be laid to rest. And the doctor—you can't take the doctor just yet. We need him. Grandfather needs him. Bianca, too, stands in need of him."

"The doctor's services," said Sebastian, "come at too high a price. I am shaking the dust of this place from my feet forever. There is nothing left for me here. Perhaps I will go abroad. Your bag, Doctor. At once."

"Nonsense," said Andelucia, and there was a thread of steel running through the word. "You are acting hastily. Rashly. As usual. We have need of the doctor. The doctor stays—"

"The doctor has a pressing appointment in town which cannot be ignored," said Sebastian harshly. "I will send another doctor the minute we arrive."

Andelucia did not remove her hand from mine. I made no move to get my bag.

Again silence, and in the silence, above the drumming of the rain and the slewing of the wind, chimes sounded.

Sebastian stiffened. "Are you expecting someone?"

"The wind," said Andelucia wearily. "You must

have noticed the wind."

"Bianca," I interposed suddenly. "Sometimes she likes to play games. The barn. The bridge. The Packard. Covers and closets. She likes to sneak up on people and surprise them. She probably snuck out the back way and is having a little fun at my expense. She's a great one for playing games."

And I felt a surge of wild hope at the prospect of seeing Bianca again, hale and hearty.

Sebastian leveled his gaze at me. "Bianca does not play games," he said. "She tries to kill people. Someday she may just succeed and I would hate for you to be around when that happens, if you get my meaning."

Andelucia smiled. "I think you fail to appreciate all that the doctor has done for us, Sebastian. Bianca is not what she was."

"I understand only too well what the doctor has done. Doctor—*your bag!*"

It was a direct order, yet I did not budge, but perhaps it was less a desire to stay and more because of the unexpected appearance in the dining room doorway of a personage in an overcoat dripping rain, wearing a wide-brimmed hat, also dripping rain.

45

"Sebastian," said the newcomer mildly, removing his hat and shaking the excess rain on the floor. His hair was the color of sand, generously sprinkled with white. The mustache was yellowed and grizzled and was attempting in vain to produce handlebars at either end.

"Inspector," replied Sebastian, suddenly expressionless.

Tension in the room thickened somewhat.

"Inspector?" queried Andelucia.

"Inspector," said Sebastian, "let me present my sister, Andelucia, as well as the doctor and our neighbor."

"Have a seat, Inspector," offered Andelucia generously. "I'm afraid we didn't hear you drive up."

"There are times," said the inspector enigmatically, "when one does not wish to announce in advance one's presence."

He removed his coat and draped it over the back of a chair. His hat he placed on a spindle of the chair. He was thickish about the waist, yet the shoulders were broad and suggested latent power. His motions were deliberate, his manner laconic, his eyes blue steel. He cast a lazy glance in Sebastian's direction. "Going somewhere?" he inquired, having a seat. "In a hurry?"

"The doctor," said Sebastian, "has a pressing appointment in town. No time to stay and chat. No time to be fetching bags. We're leaving."

Andelucia's hand restrained me still.

The inspector cleared his throat apologetically. "I received, some while ago, a disturbing call. A call—shall we say—of distress?"

"I perceive," said Andelucia dryly, "that Evangeline never made it to her room at all. Perhaps something to drink, Inspector?"

"Thank you, no," said the inspector, reaching into a vest pocket and pulling forth a notepad and a stub of pencil. "There was talk of accidents. Names were mentioned." He brought the notepad up and squinted. "Clarissa. Daphne. Bianca."

"Unfortunate incidents," agreed Andelucia. "Evangeline won't bother you again. Ever. She was a—a little wrought up."

"So I gathered," said the inspector dryly, "and yet, there are times when circumstances suggest a closer examination of the facts. An accident, after all, is not to be wondered at. Two, and the weight of suspicion begins to cast an ugly shadow. Three, and—well, here we are. Perhaps Sebastian may be able to clear these matters up by answering a few questions."

The tone was offhand, yet the command was unmistakable.

Sebastian hesitated, then drew up a chair. "I just arrived myself, you understand, Inspector. Accidents, you say? I find myself intrigued. I trust I can be of some small assistance."

The inspector shrugged. "I, too, am hopeful that you can cast some light on one or two minor points." He pulled a handkerchief out of a vest pocket and used it to draw forth a pipe wrench from inside his overcoat. He set it gently on the table.

I stiffened and forced my lungs to draw breath through the darkness that suddenly constricted my chest.

Andelucia frowned. "What are you doing with Sebastian's wrench, Inspector?"

"I was curious," admitted the inspector, "as to how this came to be lying beneath the bridge, next to a support that had been recently cut in two."

Sebastian concealed his surprise admirably, contenting himself with a flickering glance in my direction, although it was intermingled with what may have been a conclusion reached. "I, too, find myself curious," he said slowly. "Perhaps the good doctor can shed some light on this enigma."

I felt Andelucia's shoulder grow tight. "The doctor," she said firmly, "is above reproach. You may ask him anything you like."

She meant well, but her words were worms, crawling beneath my skin and eating holes into my soul.

"In time," murmured the inspector. "But it is, in fact, Sebastian's wrench, is it not?"

"Immaterial," said Sebastian brutally. "Completely beside the point. Who the wrench belongs to has no bearing. Were I you, I would be determining who had been *using* it."

"I am sure you would," murmured the inspector. "I also observed a Packard at the bottom of the hill. Could this be the one referred to by Evangeline?"

Sebastian hesitated, and then he suddenly grinned, yet within the grin was malice unmistakable. "I have no desire to interfere with your instructive and thought-provoking questions, Inspector, but perhaps these questions would be best served if directed at the doctor."

"Sebastian," interjected Andelucia tightly, "perhaps you would be so kind as to leave the good doctor out of this and allow the inspector to do his job."

"But of course," said the inspector. "The doctor again. Perhaps later I may have a few questions for him." There was a peculiar note in his voice that disturbed me.

"In the meantime, though, would you be so good as to tell me to whom this Packard belongs."

"The ownership of the Packard is hardly relevant!" said Sebastian harshly. "Your mind seems ill-equipped to grasp some very elementary and fundamental details, Inspector."

"I shouldn't be surprised," murmured the inspector. "Well, perhaps later we shall clarify some of these more obscure points. In the meantime, though, I think it might be wisdom to speak with—" He conferred with his notepad. "Ah, yes—I would like to speak with Evangeline." And he glanced about the room, as though in expectation of seeing Evangeline lurking in a doorway.

The hand on mine tightened, and for a moment no one spoke. At length, Andelucia said quietly, "There's been an accident."

The inspector glanced at Sebastian. "Yet another accident?"

Sebastian's grin broadened. "Yes, indeed, Inspector. Another accident. You have an uncanny knack for posing questions so much better suited for the doctor. Would that not be so, Doctor?"

"Shut your mouth, Sebastian," said Andelucia sharply. "Excuse me, Inspector. Evangeline is dead."

The inspector's eyebrows shot upwards. He made a thoughtful noise, then felt it necessary to add another note to his notepad. "Dead, is she? And yet, when I spoke with her she sounded quite—lively. Dead. Interesting. Four accidents. Four deaths."

"Bianca," said Andelucia firmly, "is not dead. Evangeline may have stretched a point or two when she was speaking to you. In fact, I am sure of it."

"Curious," murmured the inspector. "Not dead. I look forward to speaking with this Bianca whom luck seems to have favored. But back to this unexpectedly dead Evangeline. Most, shall we say, peculiar. Disconcerting, in fact."

"Lightning," said Sebastian suddenly. "It was lightning that killed Evangeline."

"Lightning," echoed the inspector. "But, of course. Lightning." He touched the stub of pencil to the paper. "Not the doctor this time, then?"

"Lightning," said Sebastian firmly. "There was a lot of it about. Frederick was there—he'll tell you. The doctor as well. Deuced unlucky thing. Saw it with my own eyes."

The inspector flicked a glance across the table. "Frederick, is it?"

"I didn't kill anyone," said Frederick hastily. "Sebastian says you can't kill someone by just proposing to them. He said it was just my bad luck. He said I wasn't responsible and that I should talk to the doctor about their deaths. That's why I'm here now. I'm in the middle of another one. A marriage proposal, I mean—

not another death."

"Marriage," said the inspector. "A venerable institution. The joining of two hearts that beat as one, the twining of two souls meant, from the beginning, to be together."

Frederick looked confused. "I'm marrying because if I don't marry, my money is going to be locked away in a trust fund until I'm thirty—and I need the money now. Thirty is a long way off."

The inspector shook his head. "Money doesn't last, son."

Frederick scowled. "Don't I know it. That's why I have to marry someone—anyone!"

The inspector's expression darkened, and although he appeared desirous of further speech, he did not, after all, speak.

Sebastian coughed politely. "Well, I trust I was able to shed some light on these unfortunate accidents, but now, Inspector, I really must be going."

He rose with the air of one who has acquitted himself admirably.

The inspector appeared not to have heard. He returned his attention to his notepad and made an inconsequential mark. "This Evangeline spoke of accidents. And yet, she was not convinced that they were, in fact, accidents. She used the word *murder*." He conferred with his notepad before lifting his eyes to Sebastian.

"Perhaps you would be so good as to confirm your whereabouts during the last forty-eight hours."

Sebastian's eyes narrowed suddenly and he slowly reseated himself. He leaned forward, his brow darkening, and a deliberate finger thumped the tabletop. He seemed to swell, and I was struck again by the magnitude of his presence. When next he spoke it was evident he was choosing his words with great care. "Inspector, I am growing weary of your veiled accusations. I suggest you question the doctor when you can spare a moment of your valuable time. He has been here for the last forty-eight hours. I am convinced that you will benefit more from the answers that he can provide than by anything I could say."

The inspector coughed apologetically. "Perhaps you are right, after all. Still, there is one more small thing with which you might be able to help me." He lowered the notepad and directed a piercing look at Sebastian. "If memory serves me correctly, you have an affinity for firearms. You wouldn't happen to have a gun on you, would you? Perhaps a gun—recently fired?"

A rather heavy silence followed the question, and in the stillness that followed there came the sound of footsteps on the stair.

46

The tension surging through the room took an upturn.

Sebastian stiffened. "I thought you said she was unconscious. A concussion, I believe you said. Confined, I believe you also said, to her room."

Andelucia shrugged. "Under the doctor's care, miracles have been known to happen. In fact, I'm alive today, thanks very much to him."

"So I'm given to understand," said Sebastian dryly. "Well, Inspector, I'm afraid this is where things get a little messy."

"Are you threatening me, son?"

"Just a friendly warning, *padre*," said Sebastian, back on familiar ground. "Bianca has had her brains scrambled rather vigorously. She doesn't speak. She refuses to wear clothes."

"Indeed," murmured the inspector. "This is something I should like to see. Yes, indeed. I should like very much to see this."

"Also she doesn't take much to men. Tries, in point of fact, to kill them."

"Then I can but trust," said the inspector meaningfully, with a glance at Andelucia, "that nothing untoward will happen."

"Rest assured—you are perfectly safe." Andelucia cast a sharp glance at Sebastian. "Bianca is a changed girl under the doctor's care, a fact which Sebastian refuses to accept. Ah, here she is now."

Bianca appeared, but it was a Bianca I hardly recognized. Gone the look of puppy dog affection and adoration. Gone the softness in her eyes, the gentleness in her expression. This Bianca had flecks of ice in her dark eyes and a jaw of steel.

Also, she was fully clothed. A pencil-thin tweed skirt reached to her ankles, and a twilled blouse, ruffled at the throat, flowed to her wrists.

I experienced a moment of curious disappointment.

"My gun!" uttered Sebastian hoarsely.

The gun that Bianca was holding looked remarkably like the one I had recently mislaid.

The gun was pointed at me.

I was not entirely surprised. But then, neither was I nonplused. I flashed Bianca my most engaging smile. "Hello, Bianca. It's good to see you. Feeling better?"

The thunder on Bianca's brow deepened. "Pervert!" she hissed.

I blinked.

The inspector made a note in his notepad.

Andelucia was on her feet in an instant, shaking loose my hand. "*Bianca!*" she cried. "You will not address the doctor in that manner! This is the *doctor* you're speaking to, you brainless idiot!"

Bianca waggled the gun at me. "He kissed me," she cried. "He—he ran his fingers through my hair! He thought I was sleeping, but I wasn't! *Pervert!* And all the time, *looking* at me and following me around and—and he's nothing but a *hound!*"

"This is the one who doesn't speak, then?" said the inspector. "The one who refuses to wear clothes? This—this is Bianca?"

"Bianca!" There was fire in Andelucia's eyes and granite in her voice. "You should be *thanking* the doctor! He's restored you to your—for lack of a better word—your right mind! He's tended to you and cared for you and carried you up more stairs than you can count and you will *not* treat him in this fashion! Is that understood?"

I don't believe I had ever seen Andelucia so furious. In fact, I hadn't known she was capable of such violent emotion.

"Now, put down that gun and apologize to the doctor at once!"

There was an imperceptible shift in Bianca's expression. Like ripples in a pond, perplexity and confusion moved across her face. She tilted her head, as though contemplating hitherto unknown factors.

She lowered the gun.

"I haven't been myself for awhile, have I?" she asked in a small voice.

There seemed to be a universal exhaling of breath.

"For quite some time, honey," said Andelucia gently. "For quite some time."

"I—I remember," said Bianca vaguely. "Oh, Andi—I think I remember!"

"I'm glad, honey. I'm so glad."

Color suffused Bianca's face. "I've been the most outrageous flirt! I tried to—I was with the doctor and I tried—oh, Andi! I'm so mortified. The doctor must think—"

"The doctor understands," said Andelucia.

"He was the most perfect gentleman." Bianca looked my way, shyly embarrassed and delightfully fetching. Her velvet eyes were bewitching, and she had never been more appealing than at that moment.

"I know, Bianca," murmured Andelucia. "I know."

"I wanted to kill people, didn't I? I *tried* to kill people. Frederick. Sebastian. All those doctors. Andi—I've been so frightfully *bad!*"

"It's okay, honey. Everything's fine now."

"All except for—for this doctor." Again the haunting eyes, falling upon me like starlight. "He smiled at me and I—I think I like this doctor."

"We all do, dear," acknowledged Andelucia. "He's been a great comfort to us all."

"I remember other things too." Bianca furrowed up her brow in laborious thought. "I remember an accident. There was an accident, wasn't there? Because I remember one. I was on the motorcycle and I was crossing the bridge and I remember something else, too. I remember seeing—"

"Come, Bianca," said Sebastian abruptly, shooting to his feet. "I will take you to a safe place—a place where you will not be bothered by lecherous, filthy, dirty, scum reprobates like the doctor here."

"*Sebastian!*" Andelucia shook with fury.

Sebastian held his ground. "Come, Bianca!"

"He's not those things you said," said Bianca reproachfully. "He was very nice to me. I want to stay here. With the doctor."

"Bianca!" barked Sebastian.

Bianca's jaw became set.

The inspector interceded. "This wouldn't be about the mine, would it?"

Sebastian glared at him. "Rumors," he said shortly. "Rumors and nothing more. There is no mine. There never was a mine. The mine does not exist!"

Andelucia probed her brother with a look, and when next she spoke it was in altered tones. "Perhaps not the mine, Sebastian," she said thoughtfully, "but would this have anything to do with—"

"No!" roared Sebastian, growing livid. "This is about truth and justice and getting Bianca away from that despicable monster!"

The inspector noted something in his notepad before turning to Andelucia. "You were saying? Something to do with—yes?"

"Nothing!" roared Sebastian.

"—A card game," said Andelucia wearily. "It was a game of poker, some time back. I beat Sebastian in a game of poker."

"You cheated!" thundered Sebastian. "Admit you cheated!"

"I didn't cheat, Sebastian," said Andelucia quietly. "It was just the luck of the draw."

"You don't believe in luck!"

Andelucia quirked a smile. "Perhaps, then, your loss was, in some inexplicable way, foreordained. Perhaps, in some unfathomable, unexplainable way, that game of cards set into motion a chain of events that was responsible for bringing the doctor to me."

Sebastian leaned forward and there was murder in his eye. "I'm the lucky one around here, see?" He jabbed himself in the chest with a blunt forefinger. "Me! That's who! Me! Not you, not anyone else—*me!*"

And striding across the room he grabbed Bianca by the arm, who emitted a startled shriek; Sebastian ignored her, turned on his heel, and thundered out of the room.

"*Your* gun, did you say?" the inspector called after him.

The front door banged shut.

47

It was like the calm that follows a storm, the house after Sebastian's departure. Like placid waters in the wake of turbulence.

A slight frown puckered Andelucia's brow. "I know Sebastian is a little unpredictable at times, but I don't think he'd kill off half his siblings."

The inspector offered a negligent shrug. "Perhaps it is as you say. And yet, there were a couple of responses which convince me that there is more to this than meets the eye. Something is going on and eventually I will get to the bottom of it. In the meantime, though, I owed Sebastian for a game of cards I played with him some while ago. I lost a great deal of money on that game. It did my heart good to see him squirm."

There was a glint in his eye that suggested that his thirst for retribution may not have been completely quenched.

"There's no denying that he can be a little bull-headed," admitted Andelucia. She flashed me a self-deprecating smile. "You must think mighty poorly of us, Doctor."

"No," I protested. "Not at all. I think—I think you're just—I think you're the most—"

She took both of my hands in hers and gave me a long look with her beautiful hazel eyes. The intimacy of her hands, the even greater intimacy of her eyes, took my breath away. Even now, when all the doors were closed and shuttered tight, I found myself thinking, found myself hoping—

"You know, Doctor," Andelucia said, thoughtfully conversational, "despite everything, despite common sense and the dictates of duty, I still find myself wavering. I still find myself wondering if perhaps there's another way. I'd like to think that what I know to be true *is* true."

There were times, more frequently of late, in which I had the clouded perception that she was trying to convey something of importance to me, but the words were so veiled that I could not discern the heart of the matter. Nevertheless, the sound of her voice was soothing to my soul.

"The doctor, yes."

It was the inspector, and his tone was not soothing at all. "In point of fact, the doctor is not, in actuality, a doctor."

Andelucia smiled into my eyes. "I'm not sure what you're driving at, Inspector, but whatever it is you're way off the mark. The doctor saved my life. He worked wonders with Bianca. She was right, you know. She tried to kill every doctor we had. Ask Frederick. She tried to do him in on a couple of occasions—before he learned to avoid us altogether. Bianca was, to put the matter bluntly, a homicidal maniac—when it came to men, that is. If we could understand the trauma she suffered on the bridge we might have a better understanding of her affliction; nevertheless, the doctor was able to do what others could not."

"Philadelphia Potts. No. Not a doctor. Not, in point of fact, a doctor by a long shot." It could have been that he wasn't paying strict attention to Andelucia. "He's not much of anything, really. Phil Potts. Rents an apartment in town. No siblings. Parents dead."

"He saved my life," Andelucia said forcibly.

"Nights he skims the scum off the vats at J. J. Petersen's Pickleworks. Doctor? No, I think not."

"You must be mistaken." Andelucia's voice had become taut as a bowstring. Her eyes, as they looked into mine, became clouded, and a shadow passed over her countenance. "He always knows the right thing to say. We've come to depend on him, Inspector. We rely on him. He's been a comfort to us. Of course he's a doctor."

"Phil. Tell her how Evangeline died."

He wanted the truth, but the truth was so condemning that it could not be uttered. It was useless of him to ask it of me. I could not tell her the truth.

"It was the lightning," I said. "If it hadn't been for the lightning I never would have—it was the lightning. You must believe me—it was the lightning."

It was imperative that she understand.

"Evangeline, Phil. Try to focus here, if you don't mind. Evangeline is the one with whom we are primarily concerned at the moment. Tell us, Phil. You were there. What happened?"

Andelucia was looking at me, and I was strongly reminded of the way Bianca had looked at me, out by the bridge, after I had wrapped her in my shirt. Andelucia's eyes begged me for release, for a word from me that would set her heart at ease and restore her faith.

Somewhere in the distance, an automobile engine started.

"*How did she die?*"

Ever have a moment in which your world crumbles before your eyes, and you know that, no matter how much you might wish it to be otherwise, it will never, ever be the same again?

"I shot her," I said hoarsely.

"You—you *scalawag!*" With an apparent effort of

will, Frederick refrained from lunging at me and perhaps throttling me to death, possibly because I was bigger than he was.

Andelucia flinched as though struck; nevertheless, her gaze did not waver. "You mean—shot her? You mean you *shot* her?" There was bewilderment in her voice, in the folding of her brow. "But, no—you couldn't have shot her." There was a tremor in her voice. "You've been so kind—so sweet, so wonderful. It must have been the lightning, like you said. The way you've cared for Grandfather, the—what?"

I shook my head.

"Not even Grandfather? But he was looking so well and—"

"I never gave him his medicine." My voice was thin as neglect. "Not once. Not ever. I—I'm not a doctor."

Confession, they say, is good for the soul.

They are dead wrong.

"Yes, well, he was going to die anyway. But—but you were so good to Bianca. I don't understand."

The inspector seemed to take grim pleasure in my discomfort. "You just can't tell about some people," he said, "until, of course, it's too late."

Andelucia's eyes no longer met mine. "I need to sit down," she said, and her voice was lost and forlorn.

She released my hands.

She sat down.

I, too, found it necessary to sink into a chair, and I was reminded of a similar moment in time, only instead of the inspector, it had been Daphne; instead of an empty chair next to mine, it had been Bianca—or, depending on the occassion, Evangeline. And always, always there was Andelucia.

Outside, passing before my field of vision, the Packard crawled up the hill, as though laboring under a heavy load. I felt a similar weight upon my soul and wondered if, when the occasion required it, I would even be able to rise from my chair.

"Well, Phil, perhaps you could also tell us how—are you okay?" The inspector's sudden concern was directed at Andelucia, not at me.

Andelucia moved her hand vaguely. "Fine, Inspector. I'm fine." And yet the tone of her voice, the cast of her visage, suggested otherwise.

The inspector cleared his throat. "Yes, well, we now come to Daphne. Perhaps, Phil, you could share with us how you managed to—"

Andelucia uttered a short burst of laughter, faintly hysterical. "I have the most wretched luck sometimes, Inspector."

The inspector shifted his gaze back to Andelucia. "It happens to the best of us," he reminded her. "Luck determines the roll of the die, the turn of the card, life and death itself. The Fates themselves bow to the whims of Luck."

Andelucia smiled tremulously. "I thought Gregory and I were fated for one another. I was sure of it. I developed an interest in his hobbies, in his likes and dislikes. I did my best to fashion myself into the woman of his dreams. And he—he developed an interest in our silver, our knickknacks, in anything of value that he could lay his hands on. I was a fool, loving him as I did."

"These things happen," acknowledged the inspector. "Which is why it's so important to choose wisely. Some people, you just never can tell. Phil is a prime example of what I'm talking about. Now, Phil, if you could just detail for me how you managed to—"

"And then I thought, for the longest time, that Horatio was the one. The only one for me. I was convinced of it. That he loved me for myself. I knew he had to love me as I loved him. But—no. He loved *everyone* as I loved him. Every one of my sisters were recipients of his attentions, at one time or another, including Evangeline, who was hardly at an age suitable to receive anyone's attentions. I didn't see it. Didn't understand it when it was brought to my attention. Refused to believe it when I saw it with my own eyes. I'm a fool, Inspector—a stupid fool."

"Yes," said the inspector shortly. "But it doesn't answer the question, does it? Evangeline mentioned the Packard, but she wasn't very clear as to how Phil managed to kill Daphne with it. And that, of course, is the question. How was it done?"

Andelucia gave a trembling laugh. "And then—then I met the doctor. I was choking, Inspector—unable to draw breath, the world turning gray at the edges, the next world a heartbeat away. Grandfather, Bianca, Clarissa, Daphne, Evangeline—all would be left to fend for themselves. All these things and more raced through my brain, and then I could think no more, and the world faded."

Silence permeated the room, save for the impatient tapping of someone's pencil.

"To my surprise, I awoke. Breathing. But it was more than that, Inspector. I found myself looking into the doctor's eyes and, Inspector—you must believe me when I tell you this—it was like coming home. I've never been so taken aback by anything in my life. I knew—I *knew* that our destinies were linked. Gregory and Horatio touched my heart, Inspector—but the doctor touched my soul. And then, having the doctor around the house, I realized more and more with each passing day—with each passing hour!—that my soul was incomplete without his."

The inspector cleared his throat. "Only he is not, as perhaps I may have mentioned, the doctor. This is, in fact, a point which you should probably retain for future reference. Make a note of it if necessary."

Andelucia gave me a quirky smile. "Gray hat. Gray raincoat. You didn't mean to kill Evangeline, did you, Doctor—you meant to kill me."

"No! I—no!"

"You said so yourself. You said you thought it was me. You said it *was* me. And before, under the tree—you thought it was me being proposed to, didn't you? Of course. You had no way of knowing that Daphne had decided to take my place."

"No! I *did* know! Daphne told me. She told me, so I knew, and I wouldn't kill you for all the world. It was the lightning. I never would have pulled the trigger had it not been for the lightning! You must believe me—I would never—!"

"And the bridge—no wonder you expressed surprise at seeing me there in Grandfather's room upon my return from town." Her voice became reflective. "I remember watching you there, Bianca at your knee, and thinking—thinking that here was a man I wouldn't mind spending the rest of my life with. And all the while you were thinking that your ruse had failed and that I was not, after all, altogether dead."

My anchor was gone and I was drowning and Andelucia's expression was a knife thrust to my soul.

"You've been trying to kill me all along, haven't you?" Her tone was quizzical, her eyes wretched. "Three times you tried to murder me. I didn't see it, of course.

And yet each time you managed to kill off one of my sisters. No, and I wouldn't have believed it even if I had seen it. Three times—and I was completely oblivious. No wonder the expression on your face when I introduced myself to you there on the train. You had just saved the life of the girl you were determined to kill, and I had just fallen head over heels in love with you. I am *such* a fool."

I stared at Andelucia, and her image wavered before my eyes. "It's no use," I said, and my words were hollow and without substance. "There's not a thing I can do or say." Some of the life ebbed out of me, but the words still came. "I've dreaded this moment, and now that it's here it's a thousand times worse than I could have ever dreamed. I have the worst luck you can imagine—although, now that I think on it, my financial situation has improved considerably since we last spoke. Not that it matters—Luck is probably unleashing her fury on me right this minute even though I'm just sitting here. That's the kind of luck I have. It's probably—" My eyes bugged and iron bands constricted my chest. "The bridge!" I gasped, and I gave a wild cry and rocketed from my chair and bulleted for the door.

The inspector extended his foot.

I crashed to the floor.

I lay there.

Pain exploding in my ankle.

"Running," observed the inspector, "suggests guilt. Presupposes an attempt to avoid justice. So, all things considered, running is probably not in your best—"

"Sebastian! Bianca! The *Packard!*" I said between spasms of pain. "We've got to *stop* them!"

"Yes," said the inspector. "The Packard. We come to the Packard at last. Tell us, Doctor, about the Packard. Take all the time you need. Start at the beginning and tell us—"

"Knife through butter!" I gabbled. "Flame and paper! We've got to *hurry!*"

"Knife, butter, flame—" The inspector pursed his lips. "No—no, I'm not quite making the connection. I'm afraid you'll have to explain that part over again. No hurry. No rush. Start over and try to involve the Packard in your explanation this time."

"There may still be time!" I cried. "If we hurry there may still be—"

A distant explosion suggested that there wasn't, after all, time.

"Thunder?" said Andelucia carefully.

"The bridge," I whimpered hoarsely. "The Packard." And I started to shake.

"Not Sebastian and Bianca. Not—*no!*"

"Dead!"

It was Frederick, and he was frowning deeply. "This *is* weird," he continued thoughtfully. "I proposed to

Andelucia and now Sebastian and Bianca are dead. I think maybe I was right all along and Sebastian didn't know what he was talking about. Meaning no disrespect to the dead, of course."

The inspector jotted something in his loathsome notepad. "I've seen some despicable things in my time, Phil," he said with something approaching relish, "but wiping out nearly an entire family? You, sir, are a monster!"

48

Time seemed to stand still. The rain had stopped some time ago, but the clouds still hung low and sullen. I considered asking the inspector to haul me away before I accidentally killed Frederick, but I didn't think I could move with my ankle throbbing. Andelucia could have been hewn from stone, and Frederick was moving through my line of vision, shaking with ill-suppressed emotion. "Marry me, Andelucia! Marry me and I'll take you away from this—this *scoundrel!*"

I could almost see his shining armor and prancing steed.

Andelucia's eyes became damp.

"Well, I know I'm not much," admitted Frederick uncomfortably. "But I dare say I'm a better choice than this—this ne'er-do-well. So—what do you say? You—me—'til death do us part and all that?"

Andelucia smiled the wan smile. "Thank you, Frederick. You are kind. Far too kind. But it's no use, Frederick. Despite all that he is—and isn't—despite all that he's done—and hasn't done—despite everything, I still feel—well, I still feel connected to him. On a gut level that ignores the facts and dismisses the realities I—oh, wretched girl that I am!—I love the doctor still!"

And she burst into tears.

There followed an interminable silence. The inspector seemed, for once, to be at a loss for words. He replaced his notepad in his vest pocket and tucked away the stub of pencil. Frederick was, perhaps, having trouble processing Andelucia's remarks, and as he returned to his seat his expression went first one way and then another. Andelucia had withdrawn into herself, and I wasn't sure if I should proclaim my love, or if I would be better off asking if I could borrow a gun so I could put a period to my existence.

I would have been able to think more clearly had my ankle not been throbbing so incessantly.

Incongruously, there came the sound of a step on the stair.

Frederick, roused from his thoughts, turned pale. "Ghosts," he whispered hoarsely.

Andelucia snuffled once or twice and dragged a sleeve across her eyes. "Nonsense, Frederick. You're starting to sound like Evangeline. I don't know what it is, but you can rest assured it isn't ghosts. Probably the wind. It's been rather windy today."

The inspector looked intrigued. "Is there someone around here who he hasn't killed yet?"

Andelucia tendered the inspector a frown. "I don't believe I care for your tone, Inspector. In fact, I don't think you've been very helpful at all."

Despite what I knew to be true, I found myself indulging in the hope that it was Bianca. Perhaps she had managed to escape from Sebastian. Perhaps she had come in the back way and was even now coming down the stairs. Luck owed me that much. I leaned forward, straining to see Bianca once more.

"Doctor!" The voice was strong and resonant. "I'm sick and tired of namby pamby broth and tea! I want food. Real food. Meat. Potatoes. A wedge of pie. A largish wedge of pie!"

Andelucia quirked her brow at the apparition standing before us. "Grandfather?"

There was a hint of color in Grandfather's cheeks that I had not previously noticed. He appeared taller than I would have imagined, and his eyes, instead of being bleary and watery, were arresting. He looked quite dapper in his bow tie and white shirt.

The inspector stared at me reproachfully. "Grandfather?" he said meaningfully. "I understood that you had killed him. Unless—could there be more than one of them?" Perceiving correctly that there was not, he retrieved his notepad and pencil and made a mark on the paper with unnecessary violence.

"The doctor saved him!" said Andelucia. "With the doctor around these things happen." She turned wondering eyes to me, and for a moment the unpleasantness that had gone before was forgotten. But only for a moment. Remembering, she bit her lip and lowered her eyes.

"That rascal tried to kill me!" said Grandfather strongly. "Not the doctor—Sebastian! As if I would tell him the location of the mine. The mine is yours, Andelucia—though it played out years ago. Sebastian said I was a sick man. I assured him I wasn't. He insisted I was and said he would send for a doctor, and he did, and then the doctor slipped me something because I went out like a light." A look of some confusion crumpled his brow. "Not this doctor. The other one. The first one. The one from last week."

"That was six months and a dozen doctors ago," said Andelucia.

"Six months!" Strong emotion twisted Grandfather's visage and his eyes became flint. "I will kill that boy, so help me!"

The inspector cleared his throat. "You're a bit late. The doctor here beat you to it."

He seemed to derive some satisfaction in the saying of it.

Grandfather seemed to notice the inspector for the first time. "Inspector," he said, "it's been a long time." Then he glanced at me, and there was new respect in his eyes. "I wouldn't have thought you had it in you," he admitted. "Good job, Doctor. Sebastian wasn't what you would call an asset to the community. Now—about that pie—!"

"He also managed to kill Bianca and Clarissa and Daphne and Evangeline," added the inspector, enjoying himself hugely.

Again the sharp look. "So he mentioned," said Grandfather. "Repeatedly. *Ad nauseum*. But I suspect—as would you, if you had any brains about you—that the mayhem you suspect the doctor of—that he suspects *himself* of—is best laid at the feet of that rascal Sebastian. In fact, if Sebastian were alive I would suggest plying him with questions as you would a fine wine." He clucked his tongue. "Pity about Bianca and Clarissa and Daphne and Evangeline, though."

"Well, Sebastian is not alive," said the inspector snippishly, "and the shadow of suspicion is falling heavily on the doctor, I mean Phil, who isn't a doctor at all."

"So I gathered," said Grandfather dryly. "Well, for what it's worth, I wouldn't put it past Sebastian for being responsible for his own death. He always was an unlucky chap. The only thing he was ever any good at was cards."

49

Grandfather marched unsteadily into the kitchen to procure nourishment, and a gloomy silence descended. There seemed to be a universal uncomfortableness, as though no one was quite ready to take the next step—as though, indeed, no one was quite certain what the next step was.

And then, a disturbance. A ruckus from outside.

A frown flickered on Andelucia's brow.

Frederick's eyes went to the doorway.

The inspector ceased, once more, the tapping of his pencil.

The commotion drew closer. Voices could be heard in violent altercation. Emotions stirred generously.

A peculiar expression crossed Andelucia's countenance. "Doctor," she said, darting me a quick glance, "do you believe in ghosts?"

There was a musical quality in her voice that caused

my insides to lurch. Or perhaps it was my earlier conviction that she would never, ever speak to me again. And her continued use of the title, despite knowing the truth of the matter—well, her words were tonic to my soul.

"I do!" said Frederick abruptly.

"Sit down," snapped the inspector. "There's no such thing as ghosts. Believe me, in my line of work you quickly learn that the dead stay dead and it's the living you have to keep your eye on."

The voices drew closer.

"As to your question concerning ghosts," I offered. "I couldn't really—although I'm inclined to think—actually, I couldn't say," I finished lamely.

There came the sound of the front door bursting open. There was a tramping of feet in the hall.

The dining room became bedlam.

"Andi!" yelled Evangeline, who was in the lead. Her gray eyes were stormy. "Tell them! Tell them that I get to marry Freddy! He proposed to me and I—well, I don't remember much after that, but he proposed to me and I'm going to marry him!"

She was wearing the gray raincoat and the gray rain hat, the latter torn at the temple and generously stained with blood, but beyond that there seemed to be no lingering effects of her recent death.

"Andi, tell Clarissa she has to marry Fishface!" interjected Daphne passionately, and her blue eyes seemed to throw off sparks. "She's trying to get out of it and you have to make her understand that it's her—it's her *duty!*"

"An omen," said Clarissa languidly, yet there was an undercurrent of steel in her tone. She looked regal and self-possessed in her gown, somewhat dampened but still flowing; her carriage lent weight to her words. "I awoke in the crypt and I knew at once that marrying Frederick was out of the question. You can't argue with an omen, Daphne, dear. Besides, I also have a lump on the side of my head which tells me that *you* are going to marry Frederick."

Andelucia stared at them, the color rushing to her face. "Evangeline. You're alive. Clarissa. Daphne. You're not dead." There was a radiance in her countenance that suggested she had climbed the peaks and had arrived at an earthly heaven.

A tight-lipped inspector made several savage marks in his notepad.

"Sebastian was right," muttered Frederick. "Proposing doesn't kill people. Weird. I thought for sure—but no, Sebastian was right after all."

Evangeline snorted. "Well, of course I'm alive. I didn't drink the—I mean, I wasn't—" She looked confused. "Did a tree fall on my head, because I have a gash on my temple and I think I've been bleeding quite a lot."

"I'm *not* marrying Fishface!" wailed Daphne. "He

looks like a—I'm *not!* Andi, how come Clarissa's omens only tell her to do things that she wants to do anyway? It's not *fair!* I woke up in the crypt as well so why can't it be an omen that *I'm* not marrying him? Why is it only Clarissa who gets to have omens? It's not *fair!*"

"No one's marrying Freddy but *me!*" shrilled Evangeline. "Andi, tell them—*tell* them I'm marrying Freddy!"

"Sisters!" said Andelucia sharply. "We have guests!"

A tentative silence fell.

"Now then, Evangeline," said Andelucia quietly. "What was it that you said you didn't drink?"

"Nothing," said Evangeline cautiously, her expression suddenly impassive. Her eyes flickered in my direction and she commenced edging towards me.

"Evangeline!"

There was something in Andelucia's tone that suggested dire consequences in the offing.

"I'm going to marry him, Andi," said Evangeline stubbornly. "As long as Clarissa and Daphne were alive I couldn't. You wouldn't let me. You *know* you wouldn't let me. But now he's proposed to me so he *has* to marry me!"

"It was the tea," piped up Daphne suddenly. "I'll bet it was that nasty tea she made me drink just before I went to get proposed to. It made me feel funny. It was that tea, I'll bet you anything. It had to be that tea because I feel like I've been hit by a truck."

"The tea," said Clarissa slowly, and her ethereal gaze descended upon Evangeline and it was ethereal no longer. "You made me drink some tea, too, you little wretch," she hissed, "just before I went to the bridge. You tried to kill us!"

"I did not!" said Evangeline hotly. "It was only the Sleep of Death. You weren't meant to *really* die! You only *really* died because of the doctor. I knew it was the doctor because he tried to kill Bianca as well and I didn't give Bianca any tea. Besides, the doctor was driving the Packard and he parked it at the top of the hill and it ran over Daphne and he—he had a hacksaw so maybe he sabotaged the bridge, and anyway no one was *really* dead until after *he* killed them! Only, well, since no one's really dead I guess he didn't kill them after all."

"I've been run over?" Daphne's tone was incredulous, and her hands went to her arms, her hips, her face, as if to reassure herself that she was still in one piece.

"The bridge was dropped on me?" The look Clarissa directed at me was ominous.

I stirred uncomfortably.

"What you have done, Evangeline," admonished Andelucia severely, "was very, very wrong."

"I love Freddy." Evangeline did not drop her gaze. "Clarissa and Daphne don't. I'll kill them again if I have to—but *I* am going to marry Freddy."

"Don't be ridiculous," said Andelucia shortly. "You're too young—*much* too young!"

Evangeline's chin became even more determined, and there was a glint in her eye that suggested the battle was only just begun. "Horatio didn't think I was too young."

"Oh, that Horatio!" groaned Andelucia. "I wish I'd never laid eyes on him!" She threw a despairing glance my way.

Evangeline was quick to press her advantage. "Tell her, Doctor!" she ordered. "Tell her I get to marry Frederick. Tell her I love him and he loves me and *make* her understand that I'm going to marry him!"

I blinked, unprepared for the intensity of the demand and the unexpectedness of my sudden elevation to mediator. It was an honor I neither desired nor was prepared to handle. I was uncomfortably conscious of Andelucia—and the peculiar look she was giving me.

I cleared my throat.

"Your sister is right, Evangeline," I said tentatively. "You are much too young to think of marrying anyone, and certainly not Frederick—unless, of course, you don't mind waiting a few years until you're of age, and perhaps better equipped to know your own mind."

Evangeline stared at me for a moment. Then she whirled on Andelucia. "You heard him, Andi!" she crowed. "He said I *could* marry Freddy! He *said!* He said if I wait I can marry him! I'll wait, you see if I don't! I'll wait a million years but *I'm* going to marry him!"

Andelucia's eyes lingered on mine for an inscrutable moment longer. "Yes, Evangeline—I heard him," she said gravely. "We'll just have to wait, won't we? But perhaps Frederick won't be able to wait a few years. There is the matter of his trust, honey."

Evangeline instinctively opened her mouth to protest, but then the moment passed, and during that moment the color drained from her face. "I had forgotten," she said tonelessly, and her eyes went to Frederick. "I had no right. Naturally you can't marry me. It's all over town. Your run of bad luck. Gambling debts. You have to marry someone now. Of course you can't wait. I've been thinking only of myself. I do beg your pardon, Freddy. I—I shouldn't have made such a fuss."

Her voice became unsteady, her expression stricken.

Frederick's expression also underwent a shift. His manner became contemplative. "You know," he said, as though to no one in particular, "I've been thinking. I might take a job. Make something of myself. *Do* something with my life. Might take some time, perhaps even a few years, but with something to—to look forward to...."

Evangeline trembled and her eyes closed. She drew a deep and tremulous breath and in that moment, what with the muted light filtering through the windows and the elevation of her expression, she looked almost angelic. "This," she breathed, "is the best day in the *world!*"

50

I was uncomfortably aware of Andelucia's continued gaze fixed upon me; I shifted my attention to Clarissa. Her emerald eyes were appraising me with disconcerting directness so I quickly transferred my focus to Daphne, who was eyeing Clarissa. There was a saucy tilt to her head, yet her blue eyes were glacial.

"Funny thing," said Daphne, although she wasn't laughing. "Funny thing your omen didn't know that *Evangeline* was going to marry Fishface. Funny thing, that. Kind of makes you wonder about some of your other omens, doesn't it? Like maybe the one about taking my room from me!"

I thought I discerned a look of pure venom directed at Daphne, but I may have been mistaken, because when next Clarissa spoke her tone was silken.

"Is there something wrong with the doctor?"

My ankle was still causing me discomfort, although

it was nothing compared to the discomfort occasioned by the sudden increase of attention directed towards me.

Andelucia hesitated. "Sebastian and Bianca," she said at last, "are dead."

There followed a moment of profound silence.

"It wasn't me," said Evangeline hastily. "I didn't give them any tea."

"It's an omen," said Daphne quickly. "I'm supposed to have my room back."

"Did the doctor kill them?" asked Clarissa.

"The inspector," said Andelucia meaningfully, "interfered in the good doctor's valiant attempt to save them. His was an errand of mercy, but the inspector shoved out his clumpish foot and practically killed the good doctor and the inspector should be ashamed of himself."

"It's nothing," I said bravely.

An odd expression rippled over Clarissa's features and she gave me the full benefit of her emerald eyes. "Don't move, Doctor. Stay right where you are. It might be—well, it might be broken or something. I'll be back directly."

It was an unnecessary command. I was fairly certain I wouldn't be moving anywhere anytime soon.

Clarissa left the room. Even in her haste she seemed to flow, rather than to walk. Her evening gown rippled in her wake.

"Hey!" cried Daphne. "I'm not done talking to you about omens! I've just *begun* telling you about omens! *Hey!* I'm talking to you—*get back here!*" She chased after Clarissa.

In the sudden silence that followed there could be heard a commotion from the direction of the front door.

The inspector's pencil hesitated. "Is it always this discombobulated around here?" he demanded petulantly.

51

It was Sebastian. He burst into the room, a wild look in his eye. In some respects it looked as if he had recently been on the wrong side of a fistfight. His nose appeared to be bent, blood issued from a split lip, and a bruise colored his brow. His clothing was torn and he favored one leg.

He extended an arm, shaking with emotion, and wasted no time in coming to the point. "Since you haven't put her in an asylum, I'm going to!" he bellowed.

"I perceive you survived the bridge," said Andelucia dryly.

"She nearly *killed* me! She's dangerous! If I hadn't been so quick and nimble on my feet I wouldn't be standing here now! She nearly—" The words ended abruptly. Sebastian's spine stiffened and the color drained from his face. A nameless horror seemed to overwhelm him. He spoke again, but his voice trembled, as though his hold on sanity was slipping.

"Andelucia," he said.

Bewilderment rippled Andelucia's brow. "Sebastian?"

I would have supposed it impossible for Sebastian to show fear, but he was showing it now, in spades.

Sebastian wet dry lips. "A—a ghost, Andelucia. In this room."

"You're overwrought, Sebastian," said Andelucia firmly. "You've been through a lot. There is no ghost."

"Angel. It's the ghost of Angel."

Evangeline stiffened.

"Nonsense," said Andelucia briskly. "There's no such thing as—" She checked herself abruptly. In altered tones she asked, "You mean you—you see Evangeline?"

"Gray raincoat." Sebastian's voice was strained. "Gray rain hat. Blood. See? Right there. Tell me you see her too, Andelucia."

"Evangeline," murmured Andelucia. "Back from the dead. One can only surmise," she added meaningfully, "that she's returned to haunt whoever killed her."

Sebastian swayed, and for a moment I thought he would crash to the floor.

"An omen," he said, and his voice was a transparent thing. "It's an omen, Andelucia. She knows—oh, I am found out! She knows!"

"Knows? Knows what?" prodded Andelucia.

Sebastian seemed to visibly shrink. "The bullet. The bridge. The medications and the doctors—O, Ghost of Evangeline, I swear I did not mean to kill you. Or your sisters. Killing was never my intent. I never meant to actually *kill* anyone! You must believe me! It was revenge for that blasted game of cards—and the mine, of course. I know there's silver here still, if I could but find it—but mostly it was that game of cards!"

An image sprang, unbidden, into my mind, and for a fleeting moment I saw again dead leaves cavorting aimlessly in odd corners of the crypt—where there was no breeze. Perhaps the mine was not as lost as he supposed.

Meanwhile, the inspector's lips curled into a mirthless smile. His pencil wreaked havoc upon a fresh page of his notepad.

Andelucia's expression, as she listened to her brother, was troubled.

Sebastian spoke with an effort. "The doctor's hand, perhaps, Angel—but my instrumentation. My fault, Angel. My fault entirely. It was I who killed you. I killed your sisters. Grandfather. O, Angel—can you ever forgive me? Will you not now rest in peace?"

It was a fascinating recital of misdeeds, and perhaps it would have gone on indefinitely, only there occurred an interruption.

It was Clarissa.

She breezed back into the room, a picture of elegance even with the bucket filled with supplies that she was carrying. Following closely behind her was a vociferously gesticulating Daphne. Upon seeing Sebastian, Clarissa's forward progress came to an abrupt stop, and Daphne ceased, momentarily, her chatter.

And then Clarissa spoke. Her tone was sharp.

"Sebastian."

Sebastian turned at the sound and his eyes widened. "Clarissa," he whispered. "Daphne." He seemed about to topple under his own weight. "I am undone."

Clarissa's fine brow was indicative of strong emotion. "We heard you were dead, but since you aren't would you kindly explain to Daphne about omens? Would you kindly tell her that an omen is an omen, even if we sometimes misinterpret it—hardly ever and only on rare occasions? Would you kindly get that through her thick skull?"

"Yes, Sebastian," said Daphne icily. "And when you're quite through explaining all that nonsense to me, would you kindly explain to Clarissa that not everything that happens in the world is an omen? Would you kindly try to instill some rudimentary intelligence into her empty head?"

The color seeped back into Sebastian's face. His gaze went from Clarissa to Daphne, and then from Daphne to Evangeline. "You are not, after all—no," he said heavily. "Of course not. Ridiculous. There's no such thing as—I believe I begin to understand."

"I, too, am beginning to understand," said Andelucia significantly.

The inspector poised his pencil. "Perhaps, Sebastian, you would care to elaborate on some minor points as regarding the bridge, the bullet, and the medications."

Sebastian scowled. "No, I would not!"

"Omens, Sebastian," Clarissa said. "Tell her." She knelt at my feet and unlaced my shoe and removed it. She rolled up my pant leg and removed my sock. My ankle was about twice its normal size. She gently manipulated the foot and although the pain caused me to rise momentarily, I hardly yelped much at all. Clarissa took a flannel in which she had wrapped some ice and placed it tenderly against my ankle.

"Yes, Sebastian—tell her," said Daphne, and there was in her tone a dripping sweetness that was at odds with the chips of ice in her blue eyes.

Sebastian's brow was dark—very dark. "Blast, blast and double blast," he muttered to no one in particular.

52

Sebastian seemed disinclined to talk about omens, propitious or otherwise. Fortunately, a disturbance from the direction of the front door proved a timely distraction.

It was Bianca. There was a rip in her tweed skirt that reached to her thigh; her blouse had been torn and a generous amount of cleavage revealed itself. She had lost her shoes, and her stockings were tattered. Nevertheless—and this was the important thing—she was clothed.

However, she appeared intent on killing someone, and when her eyes lit upon Sebastian this intent manifested itself to an unprecedented degree; she charged at him, snarling and clawing.

"I told you to take her away!" yelled Sebastian frantically, backing hastily away. "I told you to hang on to her!"

His words were addressed to the two strapping young men in overalls and hard hats who were in hard pursuit of Bianca.

"Leave her be," Andelucia ordered sharply.

"Are you nuts?" squeaked Sebastian. "Grab her! Get her out of here!"

Abruptly—and without warning—Bianca's rampage came to an end.

She had spied me.

My mouth was open, in the act of registering surprise at seeing the dead returned to life, but despite the utter lack of an engaging smile Bianca immediately uttered a squeal of pleasure and lunged towards me. Issuing sounds of utter contentment she curled up at my free foot and took possession of my hand.

Sebastian's jaw dropped. "She—she's mad! She's completely round the bend! She's bonkers!"

"Bianca," muttered the inspector disagreeably. "And *still* not naked." He gave Sebastian a dark look before making another note in his notepad.

"I tried to tell you, Sebastian," said Andelucia, and there was an unmistakable air of satisfaction in her tone. "The doctor has been working miracles around here. Now—would you care to explain about these young men?"

Sebastian removed his attention from Bianca and lifted a suddenly disbelieving eyebrow. "I was hoping you could do the explaining around here!"

"Me?" Andelucia appeared perplexed. "I don't understand."

"The bridge, ma'am," said the one whose name stitching identified him as Jim. He hooked a thumb over his shoulder. "Blew it sky high. Death trap. Putting in a new one. Sent you a letter."

A wry smile appeared on Andelucia's face. "A letter. Of course. What are the odds that the one time I forget to check, a letter of some importance arrives?"

"Had I not slammed on the brakes," said Sebastian testily, "we would've gone up with the bridge."

"Lucky we was there, ma'am," said Jim solemnly. "That there girl plumb knocked herself out on the windscreen. Had to pull her from the car. When her blinkers opened she went a bit nuts. Opened the boot. Chucked bricks at that there bird like there was no tomorrer. She don't speak none, ma'am, but you can't miss her meaning! She pert near kilt him!"

"Of course," murmured Andelucia. "Luck has been known to favor him from time to time."

"As to that, I couldn't say," said Jim with a grin. He held up a brick. "But it looks like he was trying to make off with the silver, ma'am—in a big way!"

Andelucia quirked her brow. "Silver?"

I recognized the brick as being one of the ones I had loaded into the trunk of the Packard, only this one was chipped, and beneath the reddish exterior there gleamed a dull metallic color.

Silver.

Bricks of silver.

"Butter!" shrieked Daphne. "New sashes!" Her eyes became electric and her body seemed to dance in place. She dashed over to me. "Thank you, Doctor!" she cried. "Thank you, thank you, thank you!"

I wasn't certain that I was deserving of her praise; nevertheless, she commenced showering my brow with kisses.

"Bracelets and necklaces and maybe a new tiara—genuine," murmured Clarissa, and her attentions to my ankle, already tender, became more so.

"'Brick by brick,'" murmured Andelucia. "No wonder Grandmother pressed the point."

"Not all of the bricks," cautioned Jim. "Just the heavier ones, ma'am."

Grandfather tottered back into the room, dabbing at his mouth with a cloth napkin. He hesitated upon seeing the increase of occupants, and then he shot me a reproachful look. "I thought I understood that you had killed him. Did you, in fact, kill anyone?"

"You imbecile!" Sebastian was addressing me, and he was upset about something. "I gave you simple instructions! Clear directions! Couldn't you even administer his blasted medications properly?"

"Sebastian," said Andelucia slowly. "I perceive that your sins have caught up with you."

"Sometimes," raged Sebastian, "I have the most *abominable* luck!"

Time slowed to a crawl. The men in hard hats had long since departed, with varying projections as to how long it would take them and their crew to put up the new bridge.

The inspector examined his notes. Apparently he found them distasteful because he ceased turning the pages and commenced drumming his fingers on the tabletop. He cast a brooding look at Sebastian. "If I had my way," he grumbled, "I'd throw the book at you and you'd rot in jail and never be heard from again." He sighed heavily. "The thing is, I'm not sure I can find a charge against you that would hold up in a court of law."

Sebastian flicked a spot of dust from his cuff. "I never really did believe in ghosts, you understand."

Through the dining room windows a shaft of pure sunlight broke through the clouds and flooded the room.

My soul, however, felt no lighter.

I knew better.

Luck was simply biding her time, preparing to lunge at me the moment my back was turned.

The minute I let my guard down.

The hopeless sigh.

Eternal resignation.

A vision of my future unfolded before my eyes—a drab and unremarkable future, stretching endlessly into a bleak and colorless parade of endless tomorrows. Grandfather no longer needed me—never had, apparently. Bianca was wearing clothes and would undoubtedly resume speaking when necessary. My services were no longer needed. Sebastian would take me home. I would return to my apartment, to my loathsome job—assuming it was still waiting for me—and life would resume its dull, tedious, uneventful, wretched cadence—

I could think of nothing more loathsome.

Andelucia looked pensive.

Perhaps her thoughts were echoing my own.

Although more than likely she was planning dinner.

The silence became deafening.

Sebastian cleared his throat and shifted his position in his chair.

"Anyone for a game of cards?"

His expression was benign, his attitude unassuming.

The inspector snorted. "Cards—with you? Have you taken leave of your senses? Cards! Or did you think we had taken leave of *our* senses?"

"I'm in," said Frederick quickly. "You can deal me in."

The inspector's brows lowered. And then he uttered the dry laugh. "Me, too. Might as well. After all—what have I got to lose?"

"Excellent," murmured Sebastian, producing a deck of cards, and there was in his manner that of one returning home after a long absence. For a time thereafter all that could be heard was the riffling of cards, the clink of coins, the—

"Well, well, well, well." The inspector sounded inordinately pleased. "My, my, my, my, my!"

"This is *fun!*" chirped Frederick.

A strangled sound came from Sebastian, and it was a sound suggestive of Justice enjoying a moment of fine irony.

"You see, Sebastian," said Andelucia gently. "It *is* the luck of the draw."

"No!" roared Sebastian. "I *never* lose! And *never* with a royal flush! I blame *him!* It's *his* fault! This is *his* bad luck—not mine!"

Andelucia slid an inquiring look my direction. "The bridge, Doctor," she murmured. "The Packard. The silver. Particularly the silver. Tell me, Doctor, for I'm keen to know—you knew of our financial situation, yet it appears you were going to—well, you mentioned a considerable improvement in your financial situation. Were you planning to make off with our silver, Doctor?"

My soul thinned itself to almost nothing. Again the sense of a rising tide, of Luck tightening the noose around my soul, of darkness with no light whatsoever. What could I possibly say? How could I possibly explain? What words were there?

I was vaguely aware that Evangeline was at my side, that she had taken my free hand and was squeezing it, as though to reassure me that she, at any rate, was for me, come what may. Daphne was still brushing my brow with kisses, and at Andelucia's words the kisses became softer, more gentle—sweeter. Clarissa, tenderly mothering my ankle, looked up at me with great warmth in her emerald eyes, warmth that seemed to suggest more than I cared to imagine.

Bianca—

The tear in her pencil skirt now reached her waist, intensifying the exposure of her creamy hip. Had the inspector not been seated on the other side of the table his hopes of seeing a less than fully clothed Bianca would have been amply rewarded, for the torn blouse now hung off her shoulder to such an extent that I found it expedient to look elsewhere. Yet in looking elsewhere I thought I saw—but perhaps I was mistaken. I had to be mistaken because if I wasn't then it suggested that Bianca was a lot more lucid this time around than she was letting on.

She had winked at me.

I wondered if waters deeper than I could possibly comprehend still lay before me.

Nevertheless, I cleared my throat.

I moistened dry lips.

And in a voice I hardly recognized as my own, I spoke:

"It may take a lifetime, Andelucia, to explain it properly, I mean."

The words hung heavy in the air as Andelucia's eyes rested upon me, and her expression was inscrutable. And then, that slow, sweet smile that could turn the darkest night into the brightest day appeared—

"Of course, Doctor," she said, and her words were somehow an angel choir in full voice, "I would love to marry you."

Thunder in my head.

Fireworks in my soul.

And then, for a time, all I was or ever would be could be found in the promise of Andelucia's beautiful eyes.

Presently, Andelucia tilted her head to one side, and the gesture was at once charming and endearing. "To answer a question you once asked of me, Doctor—yes, you have a very engaging smile."

Someone gave a derisive snort.

It was the inspector.

He lowered his cards and directed a penetrating look

at me, and yet it was profoundly apparent that he was also acknowledging Andelucia's affection, Bianca's adoration, Clarissa's tenderness, Daphne's exuberance, Evangeline's attentiveness—

"Some people," grumbled the inspector, and his tone was almost spiteful, "are just born lucky."

www.ingramcontent.com/pod-product-compliance
Lightning Source LLC
Chambersburg PA
CBHW060557310726
48982CB00008B/1153/J

* 9 7 8 0 9 9 0 5 3 2 5 0 7 *